THE HOUSE OF MARIONETTES

THE DARKLE CHRONICLES

BOOK 3

B.C. HOLLYWOOD

DARKLE DEFINITION

Dar-kle
1. To appear darkly or indistinctly.
2.
A. To grow dark.
B. To become gloomy.

CHAPTER 1
THE MORTICIAN'S LAMENT

Jack Cullinan walked the short distance from his private cottage to the main Cullinan Funeral Home building. The tranquillity enveloped him as he approached, an atmosphere of stillness despite the brisk autumn day. Crisp leaves scudded across the well-manicured lawn, at the centre of which stood a tombstone-like piece of granite proclaiming the establishment's identity. If not for it, a casual observer might think it an ordinary middle-class home. They'd never guess the building harboured the deceased in their varied states of repose.

He entered through the rear double doors, once again appreciating the structured environment inside compared to the chaotic outside world. The orderly interior was like a meticulously arranged chessboard, providing a comforting sense of structure and predictability that contrasted with the haphazard disorder beyond the walls.

The pungent aroma of disinfectants and compounds assailed Jack's nostrils and his belly performed a languid somersault, not out of revulsion, but rather an ingrained response.

His assistant, Alice MacEntee, had already suited up in her

protective gear, and a slight frown marred her youthful face. Jack noted the furrow and the downturned corners of her mouth as both were counter to her usual upbeat demeanour. Despite the grim nature of their work, he couldn't help but appreciate her dedication. Alice never shied away from even the most unpleasant aspects of the job, a trait that Jack admired.

Her cap tucked away her long auburn hair, while the shapeless protective coveralls engulfed her slender frame. Jack wondered what had drawn such a pretty young woman to this macabre profession. He paused, studying Alice's profile as she busied herself with the day's preparations. The words slipped out before he could stop them. "You're doing a fantastic job, Alice. I don't know what I'd do without you."

Alice's hands stilled, and she turned to face him, a faint blush colouring her cheeks. "Thank you, Mr Cullinan. I'm just doing my job."

"What will it take to get you to call me Jack?" He smiled to make sure she knew he was joking. "We've worked together long enough, don't you think?"

Alice ducked her head, a small smile playing at the corners of her mouth. "If you insist ... Jack."

The name sounded foreign on her tongue, but not unpleasant. Jack's smile broadened.

Alice busied herself with the instruments, her movements precise and efficient. "Oh, I almost forgot. Mum invited you over for dinner again."

Jack's smile faltered. He suspected that Alice's mother was once again attempting to play matchmaker. The woman had made no secret of her desire to see her daughter wed to the town's most eligible bachelor. Jack had declined each of her previous invitations, citing his busy schedule and the demands of running the funeral home. But he knew he couldn't put her off forever.

He glanced at Alice, who avoided his gaze. The poor girl

found herself caught in the middle, being used as a pawn in her mother's machinations. Jack felt a pang of sympathy for her.

"That's very kind of her," he said carefully. "I'll have to check my schedule and get back to you."

Alice nodded, still not meeting his eyes. "Of course. No pressure. I know you're a busy man."

An awkward silence descended upon the room, broken only by the soft clink of metal on metal as Alice arranged the instruments on the tray. Jack cleared his throat, searching for a way to change the subject.

He strode over to the motorised hoist, flipped a series of switches with ingrained motions, and watched the sheeted shape descend to the waiting embalming table. They'd done this a hundred times, but that didn't make the routine any less necessary.

"Ah, Mattie," Jack said, peeling back the white sheet. "Bit of work to do on you."

Alice leaned in, scrutinizing him. "We'll have him looking himself in no time."

Mattie's body offered a silent testament to a long life lived hard, his skin a map of faded bruises and yellowed age. They began their task with solemn focus.

Jack made an incision near the neck to expose the carotid artery as Alice mixed the chemical solution. Jack pierced the artery with a needle and fixed it in place with surgical tape. He switched on a machine and the process of swapping blood for chemicals began.

They both massaged colour back into Mattie's face and hands, banishing the pallor of death. Once done, they washed Mattie's weathered, naked body with cold water before towelling him dry. They dressed him in a pressed suit and a crisp white shirt, then lowered him into the polished oak coffin, a burial tomb disguised as a place of rest. Each step was an act of respect, masked as necessity, their movements a silent, practiced dance.

Alice, bless her careful hands, worked at Mattie's hair, mirroring the tousled style in a photograph provided by the man's loved ones. Jack took over for the makeup stage, his fingers steady against the waxy skin. He applied a light foundation, evening out the skin tone and masking any discolouration. With practiced strokes, he added a hint of blush to the cheeks, a subtle touch to restore a semblance of life. With care, he brushed a neutral shade onto the lips, sealing them with a matte finish. He stepped back, assessing his work with a critical eye, ensuring Mattie looked peaceful and dignified for his final farewell.

"There he is," Jack declared.

Alice gave a curt nod. "Aye, that's him."

Later, changed and back to the familiar world of suits and jackets without the smell of formaldehyde, Jack called out, "I'll be back for Mattie later, Alice!"

Her reply floated out of the mortuary's back rooms. "See you then, Mr Cullinan."

Jack shook his head and muttered to himself, "It's Jack, Alice. Jack."

He left the funeral home, the heavy oak doors closing behind him with a click, sealing away the silent world within. The city where he was heading, with its noisy bustle of life, would feel jarring after time spent with the dead. He took a deep breath, the chill air offering a counterpoint to the previous smell of chemicals. It was time to put on his smile, the one meant for the living.

CHAPTER 2
THE AUCTION

The weathered placard announcing the *Rare Celtic Book Auction* drew Jack like a siren's call, irresistibly drawing him through the door. A shiver snaked down his spine, a mix of apprehension and excitement that had nothing to do with the cool air of the auction room. Today was no ordinary day. This was no ordinary auction.

Jack slipped into a seat at the back, seeking a vantage point with an uninterrupted view of the room. His gaze drifted over the crowd, taking in the sea of unfamiliar faces. Anticipation hung thick in the air, the low hum of conversation punctuated by the occasional burst of nervous laughter. He shifted in his seat, the hard wooden chair creaking beneath him.

Then, as if the room itself held its breath, a hush fell over the gathered bidders. Jack's eyes snapped to the entrance, drawn by some unseen force. There, framed in the doorway, stood a woman unlike any he had ever seen.

She moved with a fluid grace, her steps purposeful and sure. Her shock of black curls tumbled over the collar of her biker jacket, the leather worn and scuffed in a way that spoke of countless miles on the open road. Torn jeans hugged her curves, the frayed edges brushing against the tops of her army boots.

Her eyes captivated him. Almond-shaped and a deep, rich brown. What untold secrets did they harbour? With a sharp, appraising look, she scanned the room before finally settling on Jack.

For a moment, the world fell away. The murmur of the crowd faded to a distant hum, the air electric with some unspoken connection. Jack leaned forward, drawn to her like a moth to a flame.

She quirked an eyebrow, the ghost of a smile playing at the corners of her mouth. Then, with a subtle nod of acknowledgment, she slipped into a seat near the front, the spell broken.

Jack blinked, shaking his head as if to clear the fog from his mind. Who was this woman? What was she doing here? Questions swirled in his mind, but one thing was certain: he had to know more.

The auctioneer's voice broke into his reverie, pulling him back to the here and now. A weathered volume lay on display, the leather cracked, the title illegible. Yet, its age wasn't what called to him; it was the strange prickling sensation at the base of his neck. *That's the one I came for,* he thought.

The opening bid, the rise of the captivating stranger's hand – these were simple formalities in the inevitable dance. The auctioneer's words, muffled by a rising tide of adrenaline, registered only faintly before his own hand shot up, a counter bid fuelled by something far more visceral than mere collector's zeal.

"Six-hundred to the dapper gentleman at the back," the auctioneer declared, his voice cutting through the hum of the room.

The woman's head snapped back, dark eyes fixing on him with an intensity that sent another tremor through him. He resisted the urge to look away, holding her gaze in defiance.

There was a flicker of hesitation, then the tilt of her chin. She was back in the game.

Their eyes locked in a silent battle as the bids climbed. Seven hundred, eight hundred, a thousand. He glanced at the book, his fingers itching to touch its ancient binding, then back at his opponent. Her eyes were a complex mix of emotions, a fierce determination intertwined with a profound, underlying fear. Yet, the resolve in her gaze remained unwavering, displaying her inner strength and resilience in the face of adversity.

His inner voice warned him to back down and cut his losses. But something feral howled in reply. "Fifteen hundred!" The words erupted from him before he could censor them, silencing the room into a shocked gasp.

He caught the flicker of fear morphing into a flare of anger in the woman's eyes before she turned, her defiance a palpable thing as she calmly stood up and exited the auction. The auctioneer's voice boomed in the aftermath, but the words meant little, the pounding of his own heart the only sound that mattered.

Even as the auctioneer's gavel fell, declaring him the victor amid a chorus of congratulatory applause, the woman's haunting gaze refused to relinquish its hold on his thoughts, her eyes burning into his memory with unsettling intensity. He'd won the damn thing, but the victory somehow felt hollow.

———

Niamh burst through the auction house doors, her facade of strength crumbling with each step. The cool rain pelted her face. The grey, overcast sky mirrored her inner turmoil, as if the heavens themselves were mourning her loss.

She stumbled down the slick stone steps, her boots scuffing against the rough, weathered surface. The distant rumble of thunder echoed the pounding of her heart, a relentless drumbeat of despair that threatened to consume her. The damp, musty smell of the rain-soaked town filled her nostrils, a fitting accompaniment to the sense of hopelessness that pervaded her.

As she reached the bottom of the steps, Niamh paused, her shoulders slumped in defeat. The rain continued to fall, sealing her fate with each relentless drop. She drew in a shuddering breath, the cold air stinging her lungs, and tried to gather the shattered pieces of her resolve. But in that moment, standing alone in the rain, Niamh felt utterly lost, her dreams slipping away like the rivulets of water cascading down the stone steps at her feet.

She'd been so close. *The Book of Ravens* had been within her grasp. But that man, with his deep pockets and infuriating smirk, had snatched it away. Tears pricked at the corners of her eyes, but she blinked them back fiercely. She wouldn't give anyone the satisfaction of seeing her cry.

A sudden caw, and Niamh's head snapped up. A raven perched on a nearby lamppost, its beady eyes fixed upon her. She stared back, her breath catching in her throat. Was it a sign?

Niamh shook her head, her curls bouncing with the motion. No, it was just a bird. A coincidence, nothing more. She couldn't afford to get lost in superstition, not now. Not when *The Book of Ravens* was in the hands of a stranger.

She leaned against the cold stone wall, her leather jacket creaking with the movement. *What am I supposed to do now?* The book was her only hope, the key to unlocking the secrets of her bloodline. Without it, she had no idea what to do. Adrift in a world that didn't understand her, hunted by the witches who sought to control her - The Sisters.

Finding the book had been pure synchronicity. She'd been researching her family name and discovered a possible ancestor from Dublin back in the late 1800s, who died shortly after marrying a Crowley. When she followed up the Crowley connection, it led her to the auction. Upon seeing *The Book of Ravens* in the auction catalogue, she'd felt a powerful connection to it. Discovering that it once belonged to Lorcan Crowley's late wife, Nemhain Murrigan, had solidified her path.

She had begged, borrowed, and stolen to scrape the cash together to make a decent bid. Not to mention the risk she took coming out of hiding; she'd spent years working minimum wage jobs in out-of-the-way towns to avoid the chance of being spotted by a Sister. *Damn him!*

Niamh closed her eyes, her mind racing with possibilities. She had to get *The Book of Ravens*, no matter the cost. She'd come too far to give up now. The Sisters were closing in, their shadows looming ever larger. She was damned if she'd allow them to recapture her; she'd spent half her life confined behind their convent walls.

But how could she get the book? The man had outbid her, fair and square. She couldn't just steal it, could she? Niamh's lips curled into a bitter smile. *All's fair in love and war.*

———

Jack paid for his prize with an absent swipe of his credit card, his mind whirling. The weathered book, nestled in a carved wooden box, was a precious prize. He lifted the heavy lid, felt the irresistible pull of the tome. Its worn cover was ancient and radiated power.

"They say it's bound in the skin of the one who wrote it."

A woman's voice, right beside him, made him jump in surprise. "Jesus!" he yelped, spinning to find her far too close.

"Oh, sorry! I didn't mean to startle you!" Her laughter was a melodic antithesis to the macabre fascination the book held for him.

"No, you're fine." He managed a shaky smile. She was even more beautiful up close.

Sunlight caught the glint of a nose ring, set off her almond-shaped eyes, danced across the curve of a full mouth. He blinked to break the spell.

An outstretched hand snapped him back into focus. "Niamh Murrigan," she introduced herself.

His hand met hers, the touch both grounding and electrifying. "Jack. Jack Cullinan."

"You're a collector?" There was honest curiosity in her voice.

"Aye. Yourself?"

"There's a family connection to it," Niamh replied, a touch of sadness flitting across her face.

"Ah." An awkward silence, but the name of the estate to which the book belonged appeared in Jack's mind like a lifeline. His face flushed with embarrassment as he asked, "You're related to the Crowley family?"

"No. It's an older connection. Generations back." Her gaze drifted to the book, a wistful expression on her face. "My ancestors were the original owners, the ones who wrote it."

"Oh, sorry, I just assumed..." he trailed off, feeling like a right eejit.

She waved away his apology with a graceful hand, flashing him a smile that transformed her from a rebel to the girl next door in an unsettling heartbeat. "No worries. You won it fair and square." A slight tilt of her head, a glint of mischief in her eyes. "What's a girl got to do to get a look at this collection of yours?"

Jack blinked again, caught off guard. A reckless impulse flared up in him, the same one that had driven the insane bid. "Maybe I can show you. Sometime?"

———

Rain pounded the pavement, a relentless rhythmic drumming. Jack and Niamh dashed across the car park, auction pamphlets held aloft in a futile effort to ward off the downpour. Laughter bubbled up in him, a strange mix of nervous tension and genuine amusement.

They reached his vintage hearse - a sombre black beast lurking amidst the ordinary cars. Jack hopped into the driver's seat, the worn leather squeaking in protest. As Niamh settled into the passenger seat, a frown creased her brow, mirroring the rain-streaked clouds above. Then, as if she couldn't bear the suspense any longer, she swivelled in her seat; her gaze sweeping across the rear of the hearse. A sharp exhale whispered through the car as she found it empty.

"Thank Christ for that!" Her features softened with relief as she turned to face him once more, a spark of mischief igniting her eyes. "You're not some sort of weirdo, are you?" she asked, her voice playful and challenging.

He paused, fingers tightening around the steering wheel. Was there any way to answer that honestly? The word 'mortician' hovered on his lips, along with darker, more potent ones.

"Well…" he began, then caught himself. He turned the key in the ignition, the hearse's engine roaring to life in a growl. Shifting into gear, he pulled away from the curb and merged into the rain-slicked street. "…how do you feel about death?"

Niamh's eyes widened. For a charged moment, the only sound in the vintage hearse was the drumbeat of the wipers and the steady drone of the engine.

CHAPTER 3
COLLECTION

The hearse pulled up alongside Cullinan's Funeral Home, the grand old building casting an imposing shadow over Jack's more modest cottage.

"You live here?" Niamh's voice carried a hint of disbelief.

"Yep," Jack confirmed. He hopped out of the car, ignoring the cold prickle of raindrops against his skin.

"On your own?"

"I do," he replied. He watched her face, a mixture of confusion and, curiously, a flicker of respect. Maybe funeral directors weren't in the category of 'weirdo' after all.

Niamh got out of the hearse, shaking her head and muttering, "You must have nerves of steel."

Jack shrugged, an oddly boyish gesture from a man who dealt daily with the final act of a lifetime. He led her toward the cottage, the patter of rain their only accompaniment.

The interior of the abode surprised Niamh. It was clean, undeniably organised, but its charm came from a timeless quality. Sleek modernity was absent, replaced instead by a well-worn comfort emanating from weathered furniture and shelves packed with aged books.

"This way," Jack said, heading toward the farthest end of the hallway.

He pushed open an oak door, revealing his hidden sanctum – an office lined with bookshelves and dominated by a massive desk.

———

The rich scent of aged wood and old leather filled Jack's office. Rows of books lined the shelves, their spines worn and weathered, seemingly whispering ancient tales of darkness and despair. Scattered throughout were macabre oddities, each one more unsettling than the last. A preserved specimen of an unknown creature stood in a glass jar, its twisted form frozen in time. A dusty antique doll with vacant eyes sat on a shelf, its cracked porcelain skin giving off an unsettling aura. An ancient artifact, its interlaced design hinting at Celtic origins.

Jack crossed to the massive glass-panelled cabinet, a fortress for his prized possessions. Placing the book to one side, he reached up and unhooked the silver chain from around his neck. Using the small key attached to it, he unlocked the cabinet and left the key in it. He retrieved the book and, with reverence, placed it in its designated spot; it fit perfectly like the last piece of a puzzle.

A soft whistle from Niamh broke the silence. "Quite the collection," she said, her voice filled with a strange respect.

"Getting there," Jack replied, playing down his pride. He closed the cabinet door, locked it, and swiftly pocketed the key. He was about to say something else when his phone buzzed with the name *Alice* flashing on the screen. "Excuse me," he muttered, slipping out into the hallway. He spoke in low tones, and Niamh thought she detected a shift to a more formal tone.

She drifted over to the cabinet, her stare transfixed on the grimoire as if it whispered secrets meant solely for her ears. With a reverential gesture, she reached out and rested her palm against the cool glass, the last barrier between her and the ancient tome. *So close*, she thought, her yearning palpable in the room's stillness. This was the closest she had gotten to the book since she first learned about its existence all those years ago.

Jack's voice cut through her musings, startlingly close. "Are you okay?"

Her eyes snapped open. "Oh! Forgive me!"

"Nothing to forgive." Jack gestured with his phone. "I have to go. Work beckons."

A hint of sadness clouded Niamh's eyes. "Ah. Okay. Can you order me a taxi?"

"Yeah, sure." Jack began scrolling through his phone, then hesitated. He met her eyes, and Niamh flashed him the most dazzling smile, causing him to blurt out, "Actually… do you want to hold on?"

Niamh tilted her head, her dark eyes sparkling with amusement. "Hold on?"

"Yes. I'll only be gone a couple of hours."

"You're not planning on taking advantage of me, are you?" she asked, mocking innocence in her tone.

"What? No! You can help yourself to what's in the fridge, and we can talk about books when I get back."

Niamh burst into laughter. "Jesus, Jack. I'm only taking the piss."

Embarrassment flamed across his face. "Oh. Okay."

Niamh crossed the remaining distance and pulled him into a hug. Her nearness, the warmth of her body against his, was a calculation, both confusing and utterly intoxicating. "I'll stay."

"Fantastic!" he managed, pulling back a little breathlessly. "But I really have to go now."

"Don't be long!" she called as he hurried through the hallway. The front door slammed, and she sighed. She turned back to the cabinet and *The Book of Ravens*. The cabinet key Jack had put in his pocket dangled from her fingers, swinging hypnotically. "Don't mind if I do," she said, a wicked smile playing on her lips.

CHAPTER 4
ACCIDENT

Jack never enjoyed driving on the dark and desolate back roads, especially at night. The trees leaned over the tarmac like grasping claws, branches scrabbling against the roof of his hearse with a rhythm that made his skin prickle. Mattie O'Brien's coffin jostled behind him, as if the old man enjoyed the ride. It wouldn't be Mattie's style to go serenely.

"One last spin, eh Mattie?" Jack muttered. At least Mattie was better company than the silent, looming shadows.

As he rounded a bend in the road, his headlights pierced the inky darkness ahead, revealing a startling sight. There, standing stark and ghostly pale in the middle of the tarmac, was a figure clad in the traditional garb of a nun - a flowing black robe and a crisp white habit. But the mask caused his heart to skip a beat – a flawless porcelain visage, its smooth surface unmarred save for two gaping cavities where eyes should have been, tiny sparks glinting in their depths like haunting embers.

Jack slammed his foot down on the brake. His own curses mixed with the screech of protesting tires. The hearse fish-tailed, headlights swiping wildly.

The vehicle careened into a balletic skid, its trajectory carrying it directly toward the shadowy, habit-clad form. In an instant, the brutal collision struck the Sister, flinging her body like a rag doll.

The hearse's rear swung around, the momentum carrying it off the road and into the ditch, where it slammed against the embankment. It came to rest with its bonnet pointing skyward at a steep angle, as if in supplication. The motor sputtered and died, but the headlamps remained illuminated, casting an eerie glow onto the branches arching above the road.

The world plunged into a half-lit stillness; the shadows lengthening and distorting the familiar into something unsettling. An unnatural silence descended, broken only by the rustling of leaves and the distant, mournful cry of an unseen creature. The air itself held its breath, heavy with foreboding. He blinked, the image of that horrid image still seared behind his eyelids. One moment, the figure had been there, the next... gone.

Jack scrambled out, nearly slipping into the ditch where the back of his hearse nestled. His legs trembled, his body overwhelmed by a sickening combination of anxiety and visceral terror. He scanned the road. Nothing. No sign of the figure he'd seen in the glow of his headlights.

"Hello? Are you hurt?"

He fumbled his phone out of his pocket, a lifeline in his shaking fingers. The tinny ring of the emergency services operator was absurdly loud, a grotesque intrusion into the vast silence of the countryside.

"Hello. I'd like to report an accident."

Somehow, the words came out steadily. Years of dealing with grief meant he'd learned to control panic, to bury it deeper than the bodies he committed to the earth. But tonight, it took an act of will to keep the tremor out of his voice.

———

Niamh had never been this close to *The Book of Ravens*. Not alone, anyway. Under lock and key, the weathered leather had an almost palpable presence, even behind the glass. Its scent, a musty mix of parchment and age, flooded her with the hint of memories both sweet and sharp-edged. None were her own.

The key she'd stolen from Jack felt heavy in her pocket. This was a desperate gamble. With a deep breath that clouded the glass, she worked the key into the lock. The hinges creaked, a mournful dirge in the quiet of the cottage. She was the worst sort of thief: one welcomed inside with open arms. She pushed the shame away.

The grimoire in her hands was heavier than she expected, its binding thick and unyielding. The book resembled an artifact, vibrating with a power beneath her fingertips, an energy that tugged at something deep within her.

She laid it open on the coffee table. Ancient markings, faded and strange, filled pages that held a faint, musty scent. Niamh traced a worn sigil with her finger, whispering the words as they came to her. It was a dialect long forgotten by many, but it flowed easily from her tongue, ingrained in memory. *Whose memory?*

A crash shattered the stillness, sending adrenaline through her veins. Every muscle tensed. Her hands closed reflexively over the grimoire, but all that followed was silence. Heavy and punctuated by the erratic hammering of her own heart.

Slowly, Niamh forced her muscles to relax. She cast a wary glance toward the rain-streaked windows, but the night pressed in, offering only dark reflections of her wide eyes.

She felt her focus being pulled back to the grimoire. Time was her enemy. Every wasted minute risked someone catching her. Yet, every symbol on the aged pages was pregnant with possibility. Each inscription drew her in, promising knowledge that might – just might – give her knowledge of where she came from and who she was.

———

Jack watched the spectacle as if from a distance. The flashing lights transformed the sleepy back road into a pulsing nightmare. The buzz of activity - police shouting orders, onlookers craning their necks, the groan of the tow truck - was a cacophony that grated against his raw nerves.

"Word must be out," the uniformed police officer murmured, gesturing at the knot of gawkers.

"Jesus, you'd think they'd never seen an accident." Jack tried to sound irritated, but there was a quiver in his voice, a tremor he couldn't quite suppress.

The hearse was being winched from the ditch. Each scrape of metal against earth set his teeth on edge. The damage looked worse up close, the sleek lines of the vehicle forever marred.

"It's not every day you see the likes, in fairness," said the police officer.

The fireman who'd questioned him earlier rejoined the conversation. "We've searched the fields on either side. No sign of the… victim."

"They wore black," Jack insisted.

"Aye, like a nun. The lamps are bright. We'd have found them by now."

The guard and fireman exchanged a look, a flicker of doubt that stung worse than any open mockery. He knew what they thought – a head injury or the shock of the accident had scrambled his senses.

"I know what I saw," he said. Even as he voiced it, the certainty in his own mind wavered. The whole damn thing felt wrong.

"I believe you, Mr Cullinan." The guard's tone was too

kind, too placating, and the poorly hidden conspiratorial wink to the fireman was like salt in a fresh wound.

"One more pass, lads!" The fireman's shout cut through the night. "Keep your eyes open. She'll be hard to see." A chorus of grumbling answered him, a wave of skepticism that threatened to pull Jack under.

"Why don't I drive you home, Mr Cullinan? There's nothing you can do here."

Mattie suddenly loomed large in Jack's mind. *What of the old man, his final journey delayed by a phantom?* "But Mattie?"

"Looks like Mattie will be late for his own funeral," the guard said. The words were factual, not cruel, but they were a cold slap that brought Jack back to this ridiculous, disorienting night.

———

Darkness cloaked the landscape as smoothly as the Sister's flowing robes. The old stonework of Cullinan's Funeral Home was barely visible, a bulky shadow against the night sky. The only light was the faint, sickly glow of the moon, casting warped reflections in the still puddles left over from the night's rain.

No human footsteps could be heard. The Sister moved with an uncanny smoothness, her body hovering inches above the ground with a faint sigh, like an old grave, newly opened.

The scent of death permeated the air, a familiar, comforting scent that most humans would reflexively recoil from. But death was as vital to The Sisterhood as breath. Their guide, their map, a tether that drew them toward their lost daughters.

Her focus was on the cottage behind the funeral home. Even without sight, she could sense the potent energy coiled there, a sharp prickle of familiar magic. The Murrigan girl. Her quarry.

The porcelain mask, its pristine white surface a striking juxtaposition against the deep, inky blackness of her cowl, appeared featureless at first glance. Yet, upon closer inspection, one could discern the yawning, empty voids that served as eye sockets, each housing a tiny, glinting pinprick of light that hinted at a presence lurking within. In truth, her vision extended far beyond the limitations of human sight, allowing her to see through the veil of shadows that others found obscuring. To her, the darkness was not an obstacle but an ally, a cloak she wielded to conceal her presence and unveil the true essence of all that surrounded her. With this gift, she could peer into the very heart of things, unhindered by the superficial facades that so often deceived mortal eyes.

She reached the cottage, the oppressive silence broken only by the whispering of her passage. The time had come. Soon, she would bring the errant witch home.

———

Every page in the grimoire pulsed with power. The experience was both exhilarating and terrifying, a seductive melody that pulled at the darkest corners of Niamh's being. The urge to delve deeper, to unleash the secrets contained within, was almost irresistible. Yet, there was a niggling fear that if she ventured too far, she might not be able to find her way back.

A sense of wrongness descended upon the room, causing a prickling unease that made her hairs stand on end. She spun, gaze searching the shadows. The window… there had been something there, a glimpse of stark white and the glint of eyes behind a porcelain mask. Then it disappeared. *Fuck!*

A faint whisper from the hallway, on the edge of hearing and only audible in the silent cottage. Niamh rose, the heavy grimoire gripped in her hands. Her heart pounded a frantic rhythm, every sense heightened.

The office door swung open with an agonizing slowness. There, framed in the doorway, stood the figure from her nightmare. The porcelain mask was horrifyingly familiar – the glow of eyes from black pits fixed upon her like a predator's. Her blood ran cold. This was no illusion.

"Murrigan... blood..." the voice rasped from the depths of the mask, each whisper grating against her sanity.

Niamh stood in the centre of the unfamiliar room, her heart pounding in her chest as she faced the otherworldly figure before her. The Sister's porcelain mask gleamed in the flickering candlelight, the pinprick sparks in her eye sockets piercing through Niamh's defences. The room itself held its breath, the air heavy with the weight of the impending confrontation.

But Niamh's fear gave way to defiance. How many years had she been under their control? How many years had she jumped at their every command? *Too fucking many!* She wouldn't go back. Not without a fight. Niamh drew a deep breath, the musty scent of the old book and the tang of impending battle filling her nostrils. Her hand lifted, fingers curling as the ancient words of binding flowed from her lips, each syllable imbued with a power that emanated from the very depths of the earth.

The Sister's head snapped toward Niamh, a snarl of rage echoing from behind the mask. With a fluid motion, she raised her own hands, her fingers twisting into unnatural shapes as she chanted in a language that no mortal tongue had ever spoken.

Niamh's guttural incantation filled the room, rising in a crescendo of raw power, drowning out the Sister's voice. A wind whipped up, unseen and unnatural, plastering her clothes against her trembling body. The Sister recoiled, then screamed, a raw, unearthly sound laced with surprise and fury.

The air between them crackled with energy, the very fabric of reality seeming to warp and distort as their magics clashed.

A high-pitched shriek, a wall of pure sound, pulsed from the Sister to hit Niamh like a physical blow. She dropped to one knee, barely keeping hold of the grimoire. She didn't pause in her chant, though. Her eyes turned black as pitch. Something shifted in the centre of the room, a darkness solidifying. It grew, a gaping void spreading outward.

The Sister's powerful shriek transformed into an enraged scream and as it intensified, the very air vibrated with the force of it. Her body contorted, malformed and impossible, limbs and black fabric flailing. For an instant, Niamh glimpsed what appeared to be a spectral female form detaching ever so slightly from the Sister, as if two entities inhabited the same physical location. Then, it disappeared, and with a last, chilling wail, the shimmering darkness sucked the Sister in completely.

Niamh collapsed to her knees, the grimoire falling from numb fingers. Her chant faltered and died. Silence rushed in, broken only by the ragged gasps of her own breath. The portal winked out of existence with a sharp clap, leaving the room untouched, save for the echo of the struggle.

Niamh didn't know how long she stayed there, body wracked with exhaustion and lingering fear. Every creak of the old cottage, every flicker of shadow, sent fresh waves of adrenaline coursing through her veins. But there was another emotion simmering below the surface – an unnerving elation. She had fought. And she had won.

CHAPTER 5
CONNECTIONS

The drive home had been a blur of blue lights and his mind spinning. Jack's hands still shook with residual adrenaline as he fumbled with his keys, their rattle against the brass doorknob sounding like a gunshot in the night's silence. Every muscle in his body tensed as he eased the door open, the soft click of the latch ominous in the quiet darkness.

He stepped inside, straining his senses. The air hung thick with the smell of old wood and dust, the usual musk of his cottage, but something was… off. His eyes scanned the hallway, searching for the source of his unease. His house keys clacked against the ceramic dish where he always dropped them.

Jack padded down the hall toward his office, the worn carpet muffling his tired steps. Each shadow stretched and shifted, his mind conjuring monsters where none lurked. He stopped at the doorway, one hand on the frame, and froze.

"Fuck," he whispered, a single syllable choked with disbelief.

His office, usually a sanctuary of paperwork and sombre formality, lay in chaos. File cabinets stood with drawers half-open, their contents spilled onto the floor. His beloved collection of books was in disarray and in the centre of it all, the oak cabinet housing his prized possessions was ajar. The space which ought to have contained his latest treasure was bare.

He reached for the key in his pocket but found nothing. "Fucking idiot!" The words exploded from him, a raw accusation against himself. *How could I be so stupid?* He lurched forward. The ornate wooden box, the only physical proof that the grimoire even existed, remained. But the worn, leather-bound book itself was gone.

"Niamh?" There was no response. *Has she robbed me?*

He crossed the hallway as he reached for his phone, fumbling for the emergency services number. In the kitchen he saw dishes glinting on the draining board, far cleaner than he'd left them. On the oak dining table were two place settings. For him and someone else? This made him pause in dialing the number.

He turned to assess the damage in the rest of the house.

Jack stood framed in the living room's doorway. Muted snoring, a soft, rhythmic rasp, floated from within. He returned his phone to his pocket.

He hesitated, one hand lingering on the light switch. His occupation existed on the cusp of day and night, of waking and eternal rest, yet even he found the thick air of this too-early morning unnerving. Jack flipped the switch to its dimmest setting.

The snoring sputtered to a stop, replaced by a groggy, sleep-laced question. "Jack? What time is it?" Niamh blinked against the sudden light and sat up, a tangle of dark curls and rumpled clothes.

His eyes briefly flickered to the forgotten tome open on the coffee table. "After two," he offered.

Niamh noticed his lingering look at the grimoire. "Shit! I found the key on the floor," she said. "I couldn't resist... Sorry."

Jack waved a hand, any hint of displeasure swept away by the familiar weariness weighing on him. "No worries. It can wait until morning."

Her dark, almond-shaped eyes darted to his face, and something in her expression softened. "Are you okay?"

He held her gaze. After a moment, he allowed a wry twist to lift the corners of his mouth. Work, funerals, life – it all blurred together after a while. Sleep evaded him often enough. But the events of the night weren't something he could explain, not easily, at least. "Just tired," he admitted. It was the truth, even if only a small part of it.

She shook her head, tousled hair tumbling about her face as she tried to shake off the lingering grogginess. Her faded and torn Sex Pistols T-shirt hung loosely on her frame, its well-worn appearance a sign of its frequent use and comfort. As she blinked away the last vestiges of sleep, a delicate vulnerability shone in her eyes, hinting at the complex emotions lurking beneath her tough exterior.

"You ate?" Jack motioned with a jerk of his head toward the kitchen.

Niamh stared at him blankly for a second, then jumped to her feet. "Yes! No! I mean, I waited for you!"

He couldn't help a flicker of amusement; the sheer energy she managed, even half-asleep, was a force of nature. It felt out of place in the quiet melancholy of his home, and yet, it was almost a relief. He was used to sombre tones and forced condolences. Sometimes the sheer messy chaos of life was more comforting.

———

Niamh tried to stifle her outburst of laughter. "Crashing a hearse?" The image of the straight-laced Jack in an accident with the very symbol of his trade was almost too absurd. It took a monumental force of will to quell the giggles threatening to bubble up again. "I'm glad you weren't hurt," she said.

Jack's easy grin faltered, a flicker of unease crossing his face. "Yeah, well, I'm just glad I didn't actually hit someone."

She tilted her head, brows furrowing slightly. "Oh?" She tapped her fingers on the table as she studied his face, trying to discern the undercurrent in his words.

He leaned back in his chair, arms crossed over his chest. "I slammed on the brakes 'cause I thought I saw a damn nun in the road. Full habit, the whole nine yards." His jaw tightened, and he stared into the distance, his unfocused gaze suggesting he was replaying the scene in his mind.

Niamh's laughter died away. A sudden chill rippled across her skin, raising goose bumps along her arms. That unease ballooned into something more, a prickling sensation at the base of her neck. Jack, seemingly oblivious to her sudden stillness, continued.

"Oh, I forgot what you said before. What was your connection to the grimoire?"

The words hung awkwardly in the space between them. Niamh's mind scrambled. "What?"

"The book. You said something about family ties?"

The room felt smaller, the air thick and unyielding. "Yep. Apparently, I'm a descendant of the author."

"Ah, witch's blood!" He forced a jovial tone. "Should I be worried about hexes?"

"I'll turn you into a toad if you don't shut up." She attempted a teasing smile, but it felt brittle on her face.

Jack laughed, knocked back the rest of his wine. Suddenly, his earlier weariness hit her like a physical force. She stifled a yawn.

"God, you must be wrecked!" He stood, chair scraping against the floor.

"A little," she admitted, unable to hide the next yawn that escaped her. "Do you have a spare shirt? Something I could change into?"

"Sure." Jack was already turning, heading toward the hall. "I'll get the guest room ready." His steps were unsteady, the wine catching up to him as he made his way down the dim corridor.

Niamh watched him disappear into the shadows, a knot of worry twisting in her stomach. The warmth and laughter that had filled the kitchen moments ago dissipated, replaced by a growing sense of unease. The house's faint, musty scent, once merely a background note, now felt suffocating, and the shadows in the corners stretched into unfathomable depths.

Standing alone in the kitchen, Niamh couldn't shake the feeling that she had made a mistake. She was a descendant of a witch, stuck in a lonely house with a man who dealt with death every day for a living. The thought sent a chill down her spine, and she couldn't help but wonder, *Why hadn't I left with the book when I had the chance?*

———

Sleep remained a phantom, skittering just beyond her grasp. As Niamh tossed and turned in the unfamiliar bed, an uncomfortable certainty grew within her – she couldn't close her eyes in this place, not tonight.

A sharp clicking sound, like fingernails scraping against glass, broke the silence. She bolted upright, heart pounding. A flicker of movement outside the window made her gasp – For a terrifying instant, a cowled shape filled the frame. Then, blackness.

Shivering, she slipped out of bed. Jack's oversized shirt hung almost to her knees and the scent of him clung to the fabric, a strange mixture of comfort and masculinity. Her hand darted under the bed, fingertips brushing the cool leather cover of the grimoire.

With the ancient tome tucked against her chest, she padded barefoot out of the room. The eerie silence in the house thrummed with a strange tension. Every creak of aging floorboards sent a fresh shiver down her spine.

Jack's bedroom door loomed at the end of the dim hallway. A thin sliver of light escaped from beneath. Driven more by instinct than a conscious plan, Niamh slipped inside.

Jack lay sprawled on his bed, his breathing deep and even. Swiftly, she crossed the room, knelt beside the bed, and slid the grimoire under the mattress on the unoccupied side. Only then did she allow herself a breath. Her next move came without conscious thought; she slipped under the covers beside him.

His warmth enveloped her. The scent of him, now familiar, offered some faint solace, but it couldn't completely banish the echoes of the clicking from the window, or the phantom nun Jack had seen, or the one she had fought. She pressed closer to him, seeking the solidity of his presence as a shield against the sense of dread.

For tonight, this would suffice. Sleep might still elude her and fear might keep her coiled against his oblivious form, but for now, she wouldn't be alone. The weight of the grimoire – a reminder of why she was in a strange house with a strange man - was a burden she would face in the cold light of morning.

CHAPTER 6
WHIRLWIND

Jack stirred from his slumber. His hand reached across to the other side of the bed, only to find it empty, the sheets cool to the touch. He sat up, rubbing the sleep from his eyes, and noticed the enticing aroma of breakfast wafting through the air, filling the room with the warm, comforting scents of a new day. The rich, earthy fragrance of freshly brewed coffee mingled with the subtle, buttery scent of toast and the unmistakable smell of sizzling bacon. A touch of sweetness, perhaps from homemade jam or honey, complemented the savoury elements.

Curious, he threw on a robe and padded down the hall to investigate.

As he entered the kitchen, Jack found Niamh standing at the stove, her back to him. She was wearing his shirt from the night before, the hem barely skimming her thighs. Her dark curls were tousled, and she hummed softly as she tended to something sizzling in the pan.

"Morning," Jack said, his voice still rough with sleep.

Niamh turned, a playful smirk on her lips. "Glad you're awake. I thought you might have died."

Jack chuckled, running a hand through his ginger hair. "Not yet."

"Pity," Niamh teased, her eyes sparkling. "I was hoping to inherit your book collection."

Jack moved to stand beside her at the stove. He peered into the pan, where eggs were frying alongside sizzling bacon. "Smells delicious."

Niamh bumped her hip against his. "Figured you could use a proper breakfast after last night's excitement."

For a moment, he didn't know what she was talking about. He recalled Niamh's presence in bed beside him but he didn't think anything happened between them. His mind flashed back to the strange figure on the road, the crash, and the chaos that followed. He shook his head, trying to clear the unsettling memory. "I appreciate it," he said, forcing a smile.

Niamh turned off the stove and slid the eggs and bacon onto plates. "Come on," she said, handing him one. "Let's eat."

Jack accepted the plate gratefully, following Niamh to the small kitchen table. As they sat down to eat, he couldn't help but marvel at how natural it felt to have her in his home, wearing his clothes. It was as if she belonged there, a piece of his life he hadn't known was missing until she'd crashed into it.

As they ate, Jack couldn't shake the nagging question in the back of his mind. He cleared his throat, trying to find the right words. "So, about last night..." he began, his face already flushing. "Did we... I mean, I don't remember if we..."

Niamh looked up from her plate, her brows knitted in confusion. Then realisation dawned on her face and she burst out laughing. "God no! You think I'm that easy?"

Jack's face turned a deeper shade of crimson. He'd never felt so embarrassed in his life. He wished the floor would open up and swallow him whole. "I didn't mean... I just wanted to be sure..."

Niamh's laughter died down when she saw the mortification on his face. "Oh, Jack," she said, reaching across the table to touch his hand. "I'm sorry. I didn't mean to embarrass you."

He shook his head, still unable to meet her gaze. "No, it's fine. I shouldn't have assumed."

"Hey," Niamh said softly, waiting until he looked up at her. "It's okay. Nothing happened. I just... I didn't want to be alone last night. After everything that happened, I needed to feel safe. And being with you... it made me feel safe."

Jack's embarrassment faded, replaced by a warmth spreading through his chest. He'd never had someone tell him that before - that he made them feel safe. It was a foreign concept to him, one that he found he quite liked.

After they finished eating, Jack's heart sank as Niamh pushed her plate away and stood up from the table. "I should be going," she said, not quite meeting his eyes. "I've imposed on you long enough."

Panic gripped Jack's chest at the thought of her leaving. He couldn't explain it, but the idea of being alone in the cottage, without her presence, felt unbearable. He stood up quickly, nearly knocking over his chair in the process.

"Wait," he said, his voice tinged with desperation. "You don't have to go."

Niamh looked at him then, her dark eyes searching his face. "Jack, I appreciate everything you've done for me, but I can't stay here forever."

Jack knew she was right. He had work to do, a funeral home to run. Mattie's body still needed tending to, and he couldn't neglect his responsibilities. But the thought of Niamh walking out the door, disappearing from his life as suddenly as she'd entered it, made his stomach twist.

"I know," he said, running a hand through his hair. "I have to get back to work. But you're welcome to stay here, in the cottage. For as long as you need."

Niamh's brows furrowed, and for a moment, Jack thought she might refuse. But then, a small smile tugged at the corners of her mouth. "Are you sure? I don't want to be any bother."

Relief flooded through Jack's veins. "You're not a bother," he said, perhaps a bit too quickly. "I mean, I'd feel better knowing you were here..." he trailed off, not sure how to finish that thought. The memory of the figure on the road, the crash, the chaos that followed - it all felt like a distant nightmare now, with Niamh standing in front of him, solid and real.

Niamh nodded, her smile growing wider. "Alright, then. I'll stay. For a little while longer."

Jack couldn't help the grin that spread across his face. "Good," he said, feeling a weight lift from his shoulders. "That's good."

He knew he had work to do, that he couldn't linger in the cottage all day. But knowing that Niamh would be there when he returned, that he wouldn't have to face the empty rooms and the silence alone, made the prospect of facing the day ahead a little less daunting.

———

Niamh cleared the breakfast dishes, her mind drifting to Jack and the events of the previous night. The grimoire's allure tugged at her thoughts as she tidied the kitchen, its ancient power calling to her. She couldn't help but wonder how long she could stay in its vicinity without overstaying her welcome.

With a sigh, she made her way to the office, the scene of her confrontation with the Sister. The room lay in disarray, books strewn across the floor and furniture overturned. Niamh set about righting the chaos, her movements methodical as she lost herself in thought.

Jack's presence was in every corner of the cottage, his

scent on the shirt she still wore, his belongings scattered about. A warmth bloomed in her chest at the thought of him, a feeling she hadn't experienced in longer than she cared to remember. But with it came a twinge of guilt, knowing she had brought danger to his doorstep.

As she shelved the last of the fallen books, her fingers brushed against the grimoire. The book was the key to protecting herself and those around her; she was certain of it. But at what cost?

Niamh paced the cottage, her restlessness growing with each passing minute. The silence unnerved her more than she cared to admit. The walls closing in as she glanced at the clock, wondering how long Jack had been gone. Part of her longed for his return, craving the comfort of his presence and the distraction he provided from her troubled thoughts. Yet another part feared the inevitable questions he would ask, the explanations she might have to give.

The thought of Jack at the funeral home, preparing for Mattie's wake, filled her with a strange longing. Before she could second-guess herself, Niamh slipped out the door, crossing the short distance to the funeral home. She felt like a burglar as she stole through the back entrance, her footsteps echoing in the empty hallway. The conflicting emotions swirled within her - a tempest of fear, longing, and uncertainty - as she navigated the unfamiliar space.

Despite her trepidation, Niamh couldn't shake the need to be near Jack. But the prospect of confronting death head-on, of being surrounded by the trappings of mourning, sent a shiver down her spine. As she ventured deeper into the funeral home, Niamh knew she couldn't hide from the truth forever, but the idea of revealing her secrets and facing Jack's reaction filled her with a dread that threatened to overwhelm her resolve.

The sound of voices drew her toward the embalming room. Niamh peered through the doorway, her breath catching in her throat at the sight of Jack and Alice working together. They moved with a practiced ease, their hands expertly preparing a body.

Niamh watched as Jack leaned in close to Alice, murmuring something she couldn't quite catch. Alice laughed and the intimacy of the moment made Niamh's heart clench, a twinge of jealousy coursing through her.

She stepped back from the doorway, her mind reeling. The epiphany struck Niamh with the force of a wrecking ball - she was developing feelings for Jack. The thought both thrilled and terrified her, the implications swirling in her mind.

Niamh leaned against the wall, her eyes closing as she tried to steady her breathing. She couldn't deny the attraction she felt toward Jack, the way he made her feel safe. But the thought of bringing more danger into his life made her stomach churn.

As Niamh pushed away from the wall, she could feel her heart racing, its thumping reverberating in her chest. She needed to leave before Jack discovered her. She needed time to confront the feelings swirling inside her.

As she turned to go, her elbow knocked over a metal tray, sending it clattering to the floor with a horrendous noise. The sound echoed through the funeral home, and Niamh froze, her eyes wide with panic. She heard Jack's voice, sharp and alarmed, calling out, "Who's there?"

Niamh took a deep breath, steeling herself before stepping into the doorway of the embalming room. Jack and Alice stared at her, their expressions a mix of surprise and confusion.

"I'm sorry," Niamh said, her voice shaking slightly. "I didn't mean to interrupt."

Jack's brow furrowed, but his eyes softened as he looked at her. "Niamh, what are you doing here?"

Niamh's gaze darted to Alice, who stood silently beside

Jack, her hands clasped in front of her. "I... I was just..." she trailed off, unsure how to explain her presence.

Jack sensed her discomfort. He gestured toward Alice, a small smile on his face. "Niamh, this is Alice MacEntee, my mortuary assistant. Alice, this is Niamh Murrigan, a... friend of mine."

Alice stepped forward, extending her hand. "It's a pleasure to meet you, Niamh." Niamh didn't know the woman well enough to gauge the authenticity of her smile.

Niamh shook Alice's hand, returning the smile. "Likewise."

An awkward silence fell over the room. Niamh shifted uncomfortably, her eyes darting between Jack and Alice. She could feel Alice's gaze on her, assessing or just curious? She couldn't tell.

Jack cleared his throat, breaking the silence. "Niamh, is everything all right? Did you need something?"

Niamh shook her head, feeling foolish. "No, I... I was just curious about your work. I'm sorry for disturbing you."

Jack's expression softened, and he took a step toward her. "You're not disturbing me. We were just finishing up."

Alice smiled shyly, and it occurred to Niamh that she had overstepped, intruding on their private moment.

"I should go," Niamh said, backing toward the door. "I'll see you back at the cottage, Jack."

She turned to flee, but Jack's voice halted her. "Since you're here, why don't I give you the grand tour?"

———

Jack led Niamh through the hallowed halls of Cullinan's Funeral Home, a place that held countless cherished memories from his childhood. The polished wooden floors creaked beneath their feet as they walked, the sound echoing off the walls lined with old family portraits. As they walked, he regaled her with tales of his youthful adventures, his voice filled with nostalgia and warmth. He pointed out the spots where he used to play hide-and-seek with his cousins, the nooks where he'd curl up with a book, and the kitchen where the comforting aroma of his mother's cooking once wafted. Each room held a story, a piece of his past that he shared with Niamh, hoping to give her a glimpse into the life that had shaped him.

Niamh absorbed, her eyes wide with curiosity as she took in every detail of the sombre yet elegant surroundings. She asked questions about the various rooms and their purposes, showing a keen interest in understanding the intricacies of Jack's profession.

As they entered the viewing room, Jack's demeanour shifted slightly. He gestured to a photograph of an older couple, his parents, displayed prominently on the wall. "This is where we held their services," he said, his voice tinged with a hint of sadness.

Niamh placed a comforting hand on his arm. "I'm so sorry for your loss, Jack. It must have been incredibly difficult to lose them both."

Jack nodded, appreciating her sincere condolences. "It was, but being here, surrounded by memories, it helps keep them close." He smiled wistfully, his gaze lingering on the photograph for a moment longer.

As they continued the tour, Jack found himself drawn to Niamh's presence, her empathy and understanding a soothing balm to his soul. He showed her the embalming room, explaining the process with a mixture of profession-alism and dark humour that resonated with her.

By the end of the tour, Jack felt a deep connection to Niamh, as if she could sense the emotions and experiences that shaped his world. As they stood in the reception area, he turned to her. "Not as strange as you'd think, right?"

Niamh smiled, her eyes meeting his with a flicker of something unspoken. "No, Jack. Not strange at all."

CHAPTER 7
THE MOTHER

n the heart of the convent of The Sisters of Balor, The Mother's office exuded an air of solemnity. The ancient desk, its weathered wood bearing the scars of countless years, dominated the sparsely furnished room. A single candle flickered upon it, illuminating the parchment before her and the intricate details of her cracked onyx mask.

The scent of incense, a subtle blend of herbs and spices, pervaded the room. The rhythmic scratching of The Mother's quill against the parchment was the only sound, each stroke weighted with significance.

The Mother paused, and a ripple of unease washed over her. The room grew still, anticipation hanging in the air. A knock at the door confirmed her suspicions. "Enter," she commanded, her voice echoing off the bare walls.

Two Sisters glided in, their porcelain masks gleaming in the candlelight. They bowed their heads in reverence.

"Mother," the first spoke, her voice a whisper, "we bring troubling news."

The Mother set down her quill, her eyes narrowing behind her cracked onyx mask. "Speak."

The second Sister stepped forward. "The Sister sent to retrieve the Murrigan girl has not returned."

A heavy silence fell over the room as The Mother reached out for the wayward Sister. A sense of emptiness washed over her, as if there was a void where the Sister's presence should have been. The absence created a noticeable gap in the seamless tapestry of their Order.

"We feel it, too," the first Sister added. "The emptiness."

The Mother rose from her chair, her habit billowing around her. She approached the Sisters, soundless above the flagstone floor.

"The Murrigan girl is proving more troublesome than expected."

The Sisters nodded, their masks expressionless yet somehow conveying their unease.

"We will send others," the second Sister suggested. "To bring her to heel."

The Mother held up a hand, silencing her. "No. We must be cautious. The girl possesses power, and we cannot risk losing more of our own."

She turned away from the Sisters. "Leave me," she commanded, not looking at them. "I will think upon this."

The Sisters bowed once more before retreating from the office, the door closing behind them with a soft click.

Alone, The Mother let out a breath she hadn't realised she'd been holding. She braced herself against the desk, her fingers curling around its edge.

The Murrigan girl was becoming a thorn in her side, a threat to everything she had worked for. And now, with a Sister lost to only the gods knew where, the stakes had risen even higher.

The Mother straightened, her resolve hardening. She would not let this setback derail her plans. They would open the gateway, and Balor would rise.

No matter the cost.

The Mother knelt beneath the gateway in the ceremonial room, deep in the bowels of the convent. She was dead centre of the protective circle; its lines scratched into the floor with meticulous care. A bowl of water sat before her, still and dark as a moonless night.

With steady hands, The Mother uncorked a vial of thick, dark liquid. It clung to the glass, reluctant to leave its confines. She tipped it over the bowl, watching as the liquid dripped into the water, each drop sending ripples across the surface. The water turned an inky black, swirling with an unnatural energy.

The Mother leaned forward, her eyes fixed on the bowl. "Show me," she whispered, her voice a command.

Images formed in the dark water, hazy at first, then sharpening into focus. The Mother saw a cottage, its windows glowing with warm light. A figure moved inside - a woman with a shock of black curls and a determined gaze.

Niamh Murrigan.

The Mother's grip tightened on the bowl's edges. She willed the vision to change, to show her the missing Sister. But the water remained fixed on the cottage, on the woman who had caused such upheaval in their Order.

Frustration welled up inside The Mother. She closed her eyes, reaching out with her mind, searching for the familiar presence of the lost Sister.

But there was nothing. Only a void where the Sister should have been.

The Mother's thoughts drifted, seeking a name, a memory of the Sister before she had taken the veil. But the years had worn away such details, leaving only the hollow shell of who they had once been. It was like trying to grasp at the memories of a newborn, fleeting and insubstantial.

She opened her eyes, staring down at the black water. The

Murrigan girl's face looked back at her, a silent challenge. The Mother's jaw clenched. She would not let this woman, this upstart witch, unravel everything she had built. The Sisters were hers, bound by blood and darkness and time, and she would not allow Niamh Murrigan to take any more of them from her.

———

The Mother sat at her ancient desk, the weight of countless decisions bearing down upon her. As she contemplated the flickering candle before her, a soft knock drew her attention. The door opened, revealing a Sister whose bone-white mask shone against the room's shadowed depths. The Sister glided forward, a figure of duty bound by the convent's walls.

"You summoned me, Mother?" the Sister asked.

The Mother nodded, gesturing for the Sister to sit. "I have a task for you," she said. "It concerns Niamh Murrigan."

The Sister tilted her head, curiosity piqued. "You have decided how to respond?"

"Yes," The Mother confirmed. She leaned forward, her elbows resting on the desk. "I want you to spread the word among The Sisters. Niamh Murrigan is not to be touched."

The Sister's surprise was apparent, even behind the mask. "But, Mother, she has the book. We must urgently retrieve it, and her, before she causes more damage."

The Mother held up a hand, silencing the Sister's protests. "No. We have already lost one Sister in pursuit of her. I will not risk any more."

"But the gateway, the prophesy-"

"Will proceed as intended," The Mother interrupted, her voice sharp. "Niamh Murrigan's time will come. But it will be on our terms, not hers."

The Sister shifted in her seat, uncertainty radiating from her. "And if she uses the grimoire against us?"

The Mother's lips formed a smile devoid of warmth. "Then we will deal with her accordingly. But for now, we wait. We watch. And when the time is right, we will bring her back into the fold."

The Sister nodded, understanding the gravity of The Mother's words. "As you wish, Mother. I will ensure the message is relayed."

"Good." The Mother leaned back in her chair, her gaze drifting to the window. The sky outside was a leaden grey, the promise of rain hanging in the air. "We have waited centuries for this moment. A little longer will make no difference."

The Sister rose, bowing her head in deference. "By your command, Mother." She turned and left the office, accompanied by the sound of a dying breath and her habit brushing against the stone floor.

The Mother watched her go, her thoughts already turning to the future. Niamh Murrigan was a complication but also an essential piece in their plan. The gateway would open, and Balor would rise. And when he did, The Mother would be there to greet him, with all the power of The Sisterhood at her back.

CHAPTER 8
WEDDING BELLS

The first tentative rays of dawn shone through the curtains, casting a soft glow on the figure of Jack in the bed. Niamh had been up hours ago, the excitement for the day ahead making it impossible to lie in.

She carried a laden breakfast tray into the room and placed it on top of her chest of drawers. Now, instead of the spare, borrowed shirt of a year ago, she wore her own soft, faded nightgown. A new sparkle glittered on her left hand - a simple band representing their commitment to each other.

With a playful grin, she flung open the curtains, letting the bright morning light flood in. "Rise and shine!" she declared in a cheerful tone.

A muffled groan answered from beneath the covers. Undeterred, Niamh yanked the duvet away and plopped it unceremoniously on the floor.

"What time is it?" Jack's voice was a disgruntled rumble, his face emerging with a grimace.

"Six," she said.

"Jesus, woman, why are you doing this to me?"

A playful smirk tugged at the corners of Niamh's mouth as she placed her hands resolutely on her waist. "You can be late for your own funeral if you want, Jack Cullinan, but you won't be late for our wedding."

He immediately burrowed back beneath his pillow.

Niamh retrieved the breakfast tray from where she had set it down. Placing it on the bed, she wafted the enticing aroma of steaming coffee and warm, homemade pancakes in the direction of Jack's refuge. "Suicide won't save you," she informed him matter-of-factly.

One bleary eye peeked out. "Pancakes?"

He sounded torn – a man wrenched from sleep but tempted by one of his favourite treats. Niamh could almost see the wheels turning behind his sleep-fogged eyes. The power of breakfast wasn't something to be underestimated.

Jack catapulted himself fully out from under the covers, the pillow abandoned in his wake. "I smell pancakes!"

This time, Niamh couldn't help but laugh. A year ago, her first night in this same room had been a refuge against the unknown with a stranger. Now, a comfortable, playful ease had taken root between them. The romance they had wasn't something from a fairytale, but it belonged to them - crafted from stolen hours during funerals and whispered conversations in the shadows. Somehow, against that backdrop, they'd carved out their own messy, beautiful slice of normal.

———

Jack devoured the stack of pancakes Niamh had lovingly prepared, savouring each golden-syrup-drizzled bite. Between mouthfuls, he gazed at his bride-to-be, marvelling at his good fortune. In just a few brief hours, he would marry this remarkable woman who had transformed his life.

"You know," he said, mischief in his eye, "it's considered bad luck for the groom to see the bride on their wedding day."

Niamh scoffed, her dark curls bouncing as she shook her

head. "Tradition is overrated," Niamh declared, her almond-shaped eyes sparkling with defiance. "I make my own luck, Jack Cullinan. And today, I choose to spend every possible moment with the man I love."

Jack's heart swelled at her words, a rush of affection flooding through him. He reached out, capturing her hand and bringing it to his lips for a tender kiss. "Well, when you put it like that, who am I to argue?"

Niamh grinned, her face alight with mischief this time. "That's the spirit. Now, as much as I'd love to stay and ensure you don't get cold feet, I have a few last-minute errands to run."

"Cold feet?" Jack feigned offense. "Nonsense. I've been ready to marry you since the moment you first insulted my taste in literature."

Laughing, Niamh leaned in, pressing a quick, sweet kiss to his lips. "And I've been ready to marry you since the moment you first showed me your embalming room. If that's not true love, I don't know what is."

With a final wink, she turned, sashaying out of the room with an extra sway in her hips, leaving Jack to marvel at his incredible luck once more. He knew, beyond any doubt, that marrying Niamh Murrigan was the best decision he'd ever made. And he couldn't wait to spend the rest of his life by her side.

———

A wave of warmth surged through Niamh as they stepped out of the registry office into the bright day. The cheers of their small gathering of friends washed over them, mingling with the shower of confetti that rained down. Her laughter bubbled up, a delightful counter to the residual tension in her shoulders. Jack, looking ridiculously handsome in his morning suit, grinned beside her, the sharp angles of his usual sombre demeanour softened by joy.

Her gaze swept over the gathered faces of those who'd borne witness to their whirlwind romance, familiar faces from the local community and colleagues from the funeral home. The normality of it all felt like a precious gift.

Niamh reached out to pluck her bouquet free from the tangle of ribbons and flowers. With a wide grin, she spun, whirling a shower of white petals toward the awaiting crowd. A shout went up as the blooms scattered, laughter and playful shrieks filling the air.

As they made for their unconventional getaway vehicle – Jack's old hearse festooned with garlands and trailing noisy tin cans – a strangeness hit her. A sudden, brief darkening, like a cloud passing over the sun, left a chill in its wake. Her eyes darted to the polished chrome of the hearse, the reflection momentarily twisted. There, on the shiny surface, the image of a cowled figure flickered, clad in black, a porcelain mask obscuring its face. But those eyes... empty, black voids that sucked in the light.

Niamh whipped her head around, the sudden glare of daylight assaulting her eyes. Nothing. Just the gentle summer breeze and the fading echoes of laughter.

An involuntary shudder rippled through her. "Did you remember the book?" she blurted out, leaning close to Jack.

"Yes, for the hundredth time, I remembered," he replied.

"Sorry," she mumbled, "it's just... we met because of it..."

Jack pulled her into a quick, reassuring hug, cutting short her worries. "Sentimental, much?" he teased.

She swatted playfully at his arm. "Oh, be quiet."

With forced lightness, she clambered into their makeshift wedding chariot. The rattle of cans and cheers followed them as they pulled away, ushering them into their peculiar, but undeniably happy, future. The image of the Sister lingered in Niamh's thoughts, refusing to fade away. It was the first glimpse of them since the intense battle in Jack's cottage. Since then, she'd studied *The Book of Ravens* obsessively and was confident she could use it against whatever was thrown her way. But she needed the book in her hands to do so. Every attempt to memorise an incantation had met with failure; the words slipped around her mind, refusing to stick.

She took a deep breath to calm herself. *Relax, Niamh. Jack remembered. Relax and enjoy the day!*

———

The door to their wedding suite clicked shut, finally granting them a sanctuary from the whirlwind of the day. The extravagant room, a far cry from the quiet practicality of Jack's cottage, felt like a cocoon of luxury. Flowers perfumed the air, chocolates enticed on a table alongside a bottle of champagne on ice.

Jack strode to the champagne with purpose, the pop of the cork a satisfying punctuation mark to this extraordinary day. Two crystal flutes filled with the golden liquid, and he turned, glass in hand, to find Niamh standing a few feet away.

"To you, Mrs Cullinan," he said, his voice suddenly thick with emotion.

"To us, Jack," she replied, the corner of her mouth turning up in that way that always sent a ripple of warmth through him.

Their glasses clinked, and they drank, savouring the effervescence and the shared silence.

Niamh set her glass down with a decisive clink and closed the distance between them. "Thanks for today," she began. "I know it wasn't what you had in mind."

His arms closed around her, pulling her flush against him. His fingers grazed a stray curl, familiar and grounding. "You're all I had in mind," he murmured against her hair, and it was the absolute truth.

A shiver ran through her. Whether of delight or some fleeting memory, he couldn't tell. She lifted her head, those dark eyes searching his. He felt, rather than saw, a shift in the room's energy. The celebratory fizz of champagne gave way to the potent charge of desire.

Niamh took his glass and set it beside her own, the gesture a silent invitation he was all too eager to accept. "Show me," she whispered. It was as much a plea as a challenge.

The formality of the day peeled away, replaced by a hunger that had been simmering beneath the surface since their very first meeting. His hands found the curve of her hip, the delicate silk of her dress barely a whisper against his fingertips. Leaning in, the world narrowing to her parted lips, those eyes alight with an answering need. The first brush of his mouth against hers was a promise, a prelude to the long, slow night ahead.

Without breaking the kiss, he guided her toward the bed, their bodies moving in perfect harmony. As they sank into the satin sheets, Jack's fingers traced slow, electric patterns along her stomach, the silk of her dress giving way to the warmth of her skin. Each graze of his fingertips, slightly calloused from years at the funeral home, sent a thrilling shiver through her body, igniting a desire that had been building since the moment they met. His scent - clean, masculine, with a hint of champagne - surrounded her, overpowering the remnants of dark secrets and spectral threats that haunted her thoughts.

Jack's eyes, usually touched with a hint of sorrow, held only a dark, consuming heat. He captured her hand, his grasp firm but gentle, and raised it to his lips. His tongue traced a slow line along her palm, making her gasp. She'd never understood those breathless novel heroines, but now, raw, undeniable desire pulsed through her.

He pulled away, a teasing smile playing on his lips. "You taste like sunshine and trouble," he rasped, and those words felt like a sweet, whispered pact. Tonight, she would embrace both sides of herself - the practical, everyday woman, and the descendant of witches - a burning passion thrumming within her depths.

Jack slipped the strap of her dress down, revealing the soft expanse of her shoulder. His tongue followed, teasingly light at first, then bolder, eliciting a soft moan that made a low hum of satisfaction rise within him. Her response - the rapid beat of her pulse beneath his fingertips, the scent of arousal sharp in the hotel room air - stoked the fire within him.

"If you ever leave me," he murmured, half-teasing, half possessed by an intensity that surprised even himself, "I'll track you down, witch or no witch."

She laughed, the sound throaty and laced with dark promise. "Try me, Cullinan."

They kissed again, devouring each other. Only hunger remained, a shared fire they would indulge in until the first rays of dawn painted the sky.

Lost in the heady rush of sensation, wrapped in the heat of their entwined bodies, they remained oblivious to a chilling presence. At the balcony window, a still figure watched. A stark white band framed the black of a nun's habit, the face an inhuman porcelain mask, the eyes hollow, bottomless voids.

CHAPTER 9
ABDUCTION

leep clung to Niamh like a shroud, a heavy weight on limbs that ached for movement. She'd tried to stay awake, to keep vigil against the shadows that lurked in her dreams, but the weight of exhaustion had been too much. Now, the world flickered at the edges of her consciousness, a disjointed mosaic of Jack's soft breathing and the muted scent of his skin.

A breeze snaked its way through the open hotel window, rustling the curtains like an unseen hand. Niamh shivered, her skin clammy with a sense of unease. And then it came – a whisper, soft as a dying breath.

"Niamh."

Her name carried on the wind. A flicker of fear rippled through her, and she shifted, trying to burrow back into the warmth of the blankets.

"Niamhhh."

The voice swelled, a hungry echo in the quiet room. A whimper caught in her throat, and her eyes fluttered open, searching the shadows for a source.

"Come to us, Niamhhhh!"

The voice was a hiss now, a grating rasp that set her teeth

on edge. Her eyes flew open, and terror seized her in an icy grip.

"Come to us!"

"No!" Her refusal broke from her in a raw shout, and she scrambled out of bed, her bare feet barely registering the coolness of the floorboards. Her suitcase lay flung open by the wardrobe, and she dived for it, frantically upending its contents. Jack's sleepy mumble of protest barely registered.

"What are you doing?" The sleepiness in his voice was laced with confusion. Panic screamed in her own head.

"Where's the book, Jack?" Her voice was a ragged plea, fingers digging frantically through piles of neatly packed clothes.

"It should be..." Jack's words trailed off into silence, replaced by a sharp intake of breath.

The whisper surged, a grating, insistent demand. "COME TO US!"

Niamh whipped around, heart pounding as she searched for the source of the unnatural voice. The balcony window stood wide open, curtains thrashing in the wind like frenzied ghosts. She stumbled toward it, breath catching in her throat, when a gnarled, clawed hand shot through the opening and seized her wrist in an iron grip.

The force of the pull sent her crashing to the floor, shoulder slamming against the window frame with a sickening crunch. Niamh screamed, the sound ripping through the room as she fought against the relentless tug dragging her toward the darkness beyond.

With a desperate lunge, Jack reached out for her, his fingers grazing hers as he tried to hold on. Amid the chaos, their eyes locked, a momentary pause that held the weight of a thousand unspoken words, until her hand slipped away from his. Another scream, raw and terrified, tore from her throat as she disappeared into the night, swallowed by the waiting horrors outside.

The sight of his empty hand shocked Jack. One moment, Niamh's hand had been there, the next... vanished, swallowed by the night.

He stumbled, almost fell out the window. The balcony gaped like a wound, the curtains fluttering out into the frosty night to mock him.

"Niamh!"

Silence. Only the rush of the wind and the blood pounding in his ears. And then, from somewhere above, her voice sliced through the air.

"JACK!"

His head whipped upward. High above, illuminated against the moonlit sky, Niamh's hands reached down. She was being dragged, impossibly fast, by shadowy figures scaling the sheer wall of the building. His mind fought to keep up, to make sense of the nightmarish sight. Black robes fluttered like crows' wings. And masks – white, expressionless porcelain, hiding eyes that gleamed with an unnerving, empty darkness. *Nuns?*

"NIAMH!"

Naked and filled with frantic energy, Jack leapt backward through the window and made a mad dash toward the door. He charged out of the suite, careening down the hallway and crashing into the opposite wall. The nuns and their captive had already disappeared over the lip of the roof, leaving him with no time to waste. With each stride, his feet thudded against the chilly floor as he raced for the exit, driven by the urgency of saving Niamh.

The rooftop door burst open under his panicked shove, the alarm shrieking in his ears. He scarcely noticed. His eyes darted wildly across the darkened rooftop, seeking any sign of where they'd gone, of what unearthly power had propelled them up the side of the building.

Nothing. Not a trace.

His knees buckled, and he sank to the concrete, a wave of crushing despair washing over him. He cradled his head in his hands, the icy chill of the ground seeping into his skin, at odds with the fiery turmoil raging within his heart.

A voice broke through the haze of his panic. He barely registered the security guard approaching, his concerned expression blurring as tears threatened to spill.

"She's gone... They took her..." The words were a ragged croak, hardly audible above the roaring in his ears.

"Who was taken?"

"My wife. They took her... Nuns. Demons. Climbing the walls." His words seemed absurd in the face of the crushing reality, and he could only choke back a sob as it all settled around him.

The security guard nodded, his expression shifting from concern to a grim kind of understanding.

"This is Jim, on the roof. I need an ambulance." His voice crackled over the two-way radio he held, then softened slightly. "Better call the police too."

———

Jack glared at Detective Tierney, muscles tensing in his jaw. Every cop had the same bland expression, the same monotonous questions masked as polite concern. He sat on the edge of the bed, the rumpled suit clinging to him.

"Tell me what happened to your wife again, Mr Cullinan." Tierney's voice was flat, an automaton reading a script.

He wanted to scream. Instead, he forced himself to stay motionless. They were looking for him to crack, to show weakness. It was a test. "I've already told you," he said.

The notebook flipped open. A manicured finger traced lines that Tierney probably knew by heart. "Yes," - the detective cleared his throat - "you said several 'white masked nuns pulled Niamh through the balcony door and carried her up the wall onto the hotel roof.' Is that correct?"

A surge of heat washed over Jack. White-hot rage masked the gut-wrenching fear beneath. "That's what happened."

"You wouldn't have taken any drugs in the past twenty-four hours, would you?" Tierney's eyes were cold, studying him.

Jack bolted to his feet. "What? Of course not!"

"No psychedelics? Magic mushrooms or LSD?"

If the room hadn't been on the third floor, he'd have tossed the detective through the damn window. "Fuck off!"

"No need for that, Mr Cullinan." The dismissive tone, the patronising assumption of guilt, was all too calculated.

He forced himself to take a slow, steadying breath. "I'll take any damned test you want."

"I appreciate that," Tierney replied, the blandness back in place.

"And while I'm taking it, you can do me a favour." The cop's fake congeniality grated on him.

Tierney's eyebrow lifted a fraction. "What's that?"

"Find my wife."

"Rest assured, we will do our best." The statement wasn't convincing. Jack had the impression that they thought him at best, crazy, at worst, guilty.

Tierney put his notebook away, reached for the door handle, and paused. "Jack?"

Jack met the detective's gaze, daring him to continue.

"Best not to leave the country. In case you're needed."

———

Jack slumped into the worn leather chair at his desk, the weight of Niamh's absence crushing him. He reached for the bottle of whiskey, his constant companion these last few days, and took a long swallow. The amber liquid seared his throat, but it was a welcome pain. Anything to dull the ache in his chest.

His other hand held a picture of Niamh, her eyes sparkling with mischief and love. It had been taken a few weeks before their wedding day, a moment of carefree joy. Now, it was a bitter reminder of what he'd lost.

A tear slipped down his cheek, and he rubbed at it angrily. He couldn't fall apart, not now. Niamh needed him. But once the floodgates burst open, there was no way to stop the deluge. His face contorted as sobs wracked his body, the force of his grief stealing the breath from his lungs.

He clutched the picture to his chest as if he could somehow hold her again. The whiskey bottle slipped from his grasp, thudding onto the carpet. He didn't care. Nothing mattered anymore, not without her.

Time lost meaning as he wept, the night stretching on endlessly. He cried until his eyes were raw and his throat was hoarse. Until the only sound in the room was his ragged breathing and the ticking of the clock on the wall.

Jack's sobs subsided, replaced by a growing sense of self-loathing. He looked down at the empty whiskey bottle on the floor, disgusted by his own weakness. How could he sit here, drowning in self-pity, while Niamh was out there, needing him?

He thought back to the night before she was taken, when she had asked him to bring the grimoire to the hotel. He'd dismissed her concerns, but now he cursed himself for his complacency. The truth was, he deliberately hadn't brought it. Niamh had spent so much time over the past year with her head buried in the damned thing. He envied it, and he wanted their wedding night to be just the two of them, without its presence. If he'd been more conscious of Niamh's feelings, maybe she'd still be with him.

The guilt and anger swelled inside him, a tidal wave of emotion he could no longer contain. With a roar of rage, he grabbed the whiskey bottle and hurled it across the room. It shattered against the wall, glass shards raining down onto the floor.

The sound of shattering glass awakened a raw, unbridled rage within him. He leapt to his feet, eyes blazing and fists clenched tight. In one swift motion, he flipped the massive oak desk, sending papers and pens cascading through the air. He turned his attention to the bookshelves, tearing them down and scattering their contents across the room.

Like a force of nature, he tore through the office, leaving a path of destruction in his wake. Under the onslaught of his fury, he tore pictures from the walls, splintering their frames. He upended and smashed furniture, reducing it to fragments with his relentless assault.

At last, his energy exhausted, Jack collapsed in the centre of the chaos. He lay there, a broken man amidst the shattered remnants of his office, chest heaving with each laboured breath. Tears streamed down his face once more, the weight of his loss pressing down upon him amid the devastation he had wrought.

CHAPTER 10
THE SISTERS

Niamh woke with a jolt, disoriented, in a dimly lit bedroom. A headache pounded her temples. *Where am I?* Then it all rushed back - the wedding, the night of passion in the hotel room, a look of horror on Jack's face as The Sisters took her.

Eyes darting around, she registered the room's details as her eyes adjusted – a child's bedroom decorated with faded drawings of lopsided houses and crayon suns. Except, beneath cheerful stick figures lurked unsettling shapes in stark black, faceless nuns with wide, glowing eyes. *My old bedroom?*

"No, no, no, no!" She thrashed wildly, panic rising. The straps binding her to the wrought iron bed frame dug into her skin. She couldn't be back in her old room. Anywhere but there. In the far corner, she caught a flicker of movement out of the corner of her eye.

The Mother stood bathed in shadow, that horrifying onyx porcelain mask with its jagged white lines facing straight at her. Even the slight inclination of the head sent a chill down Niamh's spine.

"We are glad you have returned, child." The voice

resonated from the depths of the mask, echoing and distorted in the stale air.

Niamh forced a smirk. "Delighted to be back, Mother." The sarcasm dripped from her like venom.

"Splendid." No change in that unsettling inflection.

Fury coursed through her, the fear a background hum to the rage. It was the only home she recalled from her childhood, but none of her memories of the place were happy ones. If she ever lived with her actual family, it was before that and lost in the passage of time. She yanked against the restraints, muscles straining. "If you set me free, I'll show you exactly how delighted I am."

A ghostly chuckle came from behind the mask, a sound that crawled under Niamh's skin. "I am sure you would, daughter. Perhaps, in time. When you have settled back into a routine."

The dismissal in that voice cut deeper than the restraints. Spittle gathered in Niamh's mouth; she spat, the glob landing on The Mother's pristine black robes. "You won't get away with this. Jack will find me."

"We shall see." The Mother turned, gliding from the room with chilling grace.

Frantic again, Niamh strained against the straps, her mind racing. At least she knew she was still in Dublin, although growing up in the convent had felt like living in a world apart. Still, the familiarity gave her some hope. She'd escaped the place once, many years ago. She was sure she could again. What was different this time was she was no longer alone in the world. Jack was her family now and he would search for her, she was sure of it. *Jack. Please, find me.*

———

Jack walked into the drab interrogation room like a man condemned to the executioner's chair. One month. An entire month of the same questions, the same veiled accusations, the same dead-end searches.

"Thanks for coming, Mr Cullinan." Detective Tierney sounded sincere as ever, but Jack knew better. It was a deliberate act to disarm him.

"It's Jack. Please," he replied, the formality a thin layer of defiance.

Tierney's smile was practiced, patronising. "Jack, it is."

"Have you any news?" A surge of desperate hope bubbled up, only to be crushed in the next breath.

Tierney shook his head, and the hollow thud echoed in Jack's chest. "No, Jack. We've hit a bit of a dead end in our inquiries."

"What do you mean? I thought-" The words caught in his throat, a lump of grief threatening to choke him.

"We're no closer to finding your wife than we were a month ago." Tierney's voice was gentle, almost apologetic, which infuriated Jack even more.

An unfamiliar voice disturbed the stifling air. "Cut the shit, Cullinan. We know you did it."

Jack whipped around. Another man stared at him with undisguised hostility. "What?" He turned back to Tierney. "Who the fuck is he?"

"This is Detective Maguire. He's joining the investigation." Tierney's casual tone gave nothing away.

The new detective – Maguire – glared, a silent threat hanging heavy in the air. "Aye. And I always get my man."

The absurdity of it all was overwhelming. Jack stared at them, a brittle laugh tearing from his throat. "Jesus fucking Christ! The state of the pair of you."

He stood, chair scraping against the cracked linoleum. He needed out of this prison of doubt and incompetence. "Charge me or leave me the fuck alone." The contempt in his voice was a weapon against their disbelief. "Useless cunts!"

He spat the words and left the room, the slam of the door his final, defiant act.

———

Detective Tierney watched the door slam shut, the echo of Cullinan's frustrated exit ringing in his ears. Beside him, Maguire shifted, a scowl marring his youthful features.

"That went well," Maguire said, sarcasm dripping from each word.

Tierney sighed. "I think you overdid the 'bad cop' thing a bit." He'd been playing the 'reasonable' one, trying to build a rapport with Cullinan, but Maguire had bulldozed right through that.

Maguire shrugged, unrepentant. "Nah. Had to try something. Guy's not gonna crack with you whispering sweet nothings."

"Do you think he did it?" The question hung between them. Cullinan's grief was genuine, but grief could mask a multitude of sins.

Maguire snorted. "No, not the type. Too obvious. If he did, it wouldn't be some batshit crazy story like... what was it? Nuns?"

The absurdity of the whole thing almost made Tierney laugh. "What, then?" The case was a dead end wrapped in a riddle inside this damned missing person's report.

"Fucked if I know. Traffickers?" Maguire's voice was doubtful, the theory flimsy at best.

"Who knows?" Tierney ran a hand over his stubble. It had been a long month.

"More likely than a bunch of fuckin' penguins." Maguire snorted again.

"Aye, true," Tierney conceded.

CHAPTER 11
DESCENT

The drab grey tracksuit fell to the floor in a forgotten heap. Niamh shivered as she slipped the equally unflattering nightshirt over her head, the thin fabric a poor shield against the convent's persistent chill. The Sister watched silently, her presence a crushing weight in the room.

Another dull day at the convent had ended. A day that melded into all the others, leaving her with only a vague grasp of time passing. *How long have I been here?* She had no way of knowing.

As she tugged the nightshirt down, a strange tingling sensation drew her eyes downward. Her belly... it was swollen, a subtle curve disrupting the flat line of her usually toned stomach. Fear snaked through her as she ran a tentative hand over the swell. Her fingers grazed her breast, and she recoiled. A jolt of pain shot through her, the nipple achingly sensitive.

Eyes wide, Niamh stared at her reflection in the grimy mirror above the sink. Her period was long overdue, but she'd put that down to the stress of her current situation. *No. Impossible,* she thought. Yet, the evidence lay in the gentle swell of her stomach, in the tenderness that was entirely out of the ordinary.

"Fuck!" It was a strangled whisper, a curse, and a dawning realisation all at once.

The Sister shuffled forward, a distorted parody of a caring nurse. Her hand reached out, bony fingers like gnarled branches, toward Niamh's belly.

"Blood!" The word slithered from the Sister's hidden lips, half hiss, half croak.

Niamh slapped the hand away, disgust twisting in her gut. This... creature, this mockery of motherhood, touching her. The thought sickened her. With trembling hands, she finished fastening the nightshirt, a flimsy barrier against the horrors encroaching on every side. They had taken everything from her, her life, her freedom... and now they were intent on claiming her body too.

———

Shadows danced in the room's corner, cloaking The Mother in a sinister shroud. Only the faint, sickly glow of the bedside lamp revealed her presence as she glided across the worn floorboards.

Niamh slept, her steady breaths a subtle disturbance to the chilling silence. With a slow, fluid motion, The Mother reached toward the bed. Her twisted hand, veined and knotted like an ancient root, pulled the sheet down with maddening slowness, exposing Niamh's vulnerable form.

The change in temperature was slight, but Niamh shivered, an unconscious protest against intrusion. Undeterred, The Mother's hand hovered above the swell of Niamh's belly, and then, a feather-light caress.

Niamh stirred, a groan escaping her lips. "Such a blessing," The Mother whispered, the reverence in her voice sending a shiver through Niamh's sleeping form.

Niamh's eyes opened, first a sliver, then a startled widening. "What the fuck?" Disbelief mingled with the remnants of sleep-induced confusion in her voice.

She shoved The Mother's hand away, scrambling backward until she crouched on the pillow at the head of the bed, a feral creature defending her territory. "What are you doing?" The question hung heavy in the charged space between them.

"You must remain calm, daughter." The Mother's voice held an infuriating serenity, a calmness born of power and utter conviction. Her masked face tilted, directing Niamh's attention downward. "We don't want to harm the seed."

"Leave me alone," Niamh spat, her defiance tinged with a flicker of dread. What monstrous game were they playing now?

———

Alice MacEntee watched from the edge of the overgrown lawn, her heart heavy with concern. Jack lay strapped to the gurney, a dishevelled figure mirroring the emptiness of his gutted home visible through the shattered windows of his cottage.

The paramedics moved with a muted efficiency, their practiced routine a jarring contrast to the surrounding chaos. Jack, once vibrant and cynical, was now reduced to a shell of his former self, his eyes wild and hollowed. Unshaven and unkempt, he was nothing like the man she looked up to.

Calling the authorities had been Alice's last resort after days of failed attempts to reach Jack. The worried texts and unanswered calls had gnawed at her. This morning, the sight of doors hanging from broken hinges and the faint sounds of muffled destruction had finally pushed her to take action, her fear for Jack's well-being outweighing any hesitation.

Now guilt clawed at her. Had she pushed too hard? Her

questions, her desperate pleas for answers, had only driven him deeper into this private darkness. She'd wanted to help, had been so certain she was the one friend who could get through his grief-fuelled isolation. But now…

One paramedic glanced her way, a flicker of pity softening the professional mask. She averted her gaze, shame and help-lessness burning in her. They manoeuvred Jack into the ambulance, the doors closing with a dull thud that echoed the finality of his breakdown.

Alice was alone. She hadn't saved Jack. She hadn't even known how badly he was spiralling until it was too late.

CHAPTER 12
ROCK BOTTOM

The tray of gruel-like slop appeared – a daily ritual filled with dread. Niamh eyed it with disgust, a wave of nausea threatening to overpower her. She would not break, would not cede this last piece of control to her captors.

With a defiant set of her jaw, she shoved the tray away. It scraped against tile with a screech that echoed in the bare room.

The Sister glided forward. "Eat!" The command was guttural, a harsh rasp in the silence.

Fury surged through Niamh, overriding the gnawing hunger and constant chill. With a savage flick of her wrist, she overturned the tray. Porcelain shattered, and the unidentifiable mush splattered across the floor.

"I'd rather starve!" The words were a battle cry, a declaration of defiance.

The Sister glided a step closer, skeletal hands curled into fists. This was the moment, Niamh knew, it would become a fight for survival.

She tensed, every muscle coiled. Despite the growing bulge at her belly, despite the fatigue that seeped into her bones, she would not yield. They might have her body confined, but they would never have her spirit.

———

Their arrival was quick. Three Sisters, a silent force dressed in their dark habits. The fight that raged within Niamh faltered, replaced by a gut-churning terror. She knew what was coming, had felt the inevitability in her bones.

Hands, shockingly strong for withered and aged flesh, pinned her. A harsh grip against her jaw yanked her mouth open. The rubber tube snaked down her throat, a sickening intrusion that triggered a desperate gag reflex. Tears mixed with spittle streamed down her face, hot against the clammy chill of her skin.

The third Sister appeared, holding a jug filled with a sickly yellow sludge. It sloshed into the waiting funnel, a mocking parody of sustenance. Niamh bucked, her struggles growing weaker with each passing second.

This was no longer a battle; it was an assault. Each slurping swallow, each gag, was a fresh defeat. Her body, her defiance - they meant nothing. She was simply the vessel for whatever unholy purpose the convent served. The fight drained out of her, replaced by a cold despair far more frightening than the physical violation. They reduced her to nothing more than a womb.

———

Jack stared vacantly at the images moving across the small screen. The world existed at a remove. His hospital room was a padded cocoon, every sharp edge and potential hazard softened, muted. He sat, a fleshy lump in a threadbare armchair, and stared at a flickering television screen. The images – a vapid sitcom, a garish game show – washed over him, a meaningless torrent of noise and colour that held no purchase in his numbed mind.

No tears remained to cry, nor rage to fuel his broken spirit. The doctors had done their best, or perhaps their worst, pumping him full of sedatives and mood stabilisers. His anger had been a hurricane, thrashing against the injustice of Niamh's disappearance, but now, even that destructive force was tamed, leaving him a hollow echo of a man.

Other patients milled about, some muttering to themselves, some locked in their own silent worlds. There was a kinship in their brokenness, a shared understanding he had yet to articulate even to himself. He was one of them now – unhinged, unreliable, a danger to himself and others. Cullinan, the mortician who couldn't even keep hold of his own wife.

The flicker of a laugh track from the television jolted him. He felt as though he were watching himself from a great distance, an outside observer of this pathetic charade of existence. This was what rock bottom looked like, he supposed. And, terrifyingly, he had no will left to climb out of this chasm of despair.

CHAPTER 13
DEFEAT

Niamh sat hunched on the rough wooden bench, her seven-month-pregnant belly a burden she could no longer ignore. Shaking, she drew a deep breath into her tired lungs, savouring the sharp bite of fresh air. It was a luxury rarely afforded, these brief forays into the walled courtyard under the hawkish gaze of a vigilant Sister.

The Sister hovered nearby, a spectre of judgment that never faded from view. Niamh felt the weight of those scrutinising eyes on her with every laboured step.

"It is time." The Sister's voice was a harsh rasp, breaking the quiet.

Weariness washed over Niamh. This was it. The final chapter in her imprisonment was about to begin. With a sigh, she pushed herself to her feet. Each movement was a small assertion of will against the bleakness that threatened to engulf her.

As she moved toward the convent doors, the knowledge settled within her, cold and heavy. They had force-fed her, broken her, treated her as nothing more than an incubator.

Niamh's heart leapt at the sudden caw of a raven perched

on the roof's corner. She peered up at it, her dark eyes meeting its black beads.

"How goes it, little brother?" she asked.

The raven cawed its response, its inky wings flapping against the grey sky. In that fleeting moment, a spark of strength ignited within her, a flicker of hope amidst the despair that had become her constant companion.

The Sister's reaction was swift and predictable. With a flap of her habit, she waved her arms at the bird as if shooing away an unwelcome intruder. Niamh couldn't suppress the laugh that bubbled up from her throat. The sight of the Sister flailing like a scarecrow in a field was too absurd, too out of place in the onerous gloom of the convent.

The raven's presence had awoken something in Niamh, a glimmer of her old self. She felt a rush of gratitude toward the bird, this unexpected ally in her darkest hour.

"Thank you, little brother," she whispered.

The Sister's head snapped toward her, but Niamh met her gaze unflinchingly, a small smile playing on her lips. After months of solitude, a sense of connection washed over her, reminding her that a world still existed beyond the stone walls.

As the raven took flight, Niamh watched it soar, carrying with it a piece of her renewed spirit. She knew the road ahead would be hard, but in that moment, she allowed herself to believe that perhaps, just perhaps, there was still hope for her and the life growing within her.

———

Cullinan's Funeral Home, once pristine, now mirrored Jack's own state of disarray. The gates were closed and the grounds were overgrown and untended, an air of abandonment clinging to the building like a shroud. In the driveway, Jack's vintage hearse, normally polished to a high shine, sat forlorn and dusty, a painful echo of the abrupt halt in his life.

Jack stumbled through the front door of his cottage, the familiar scent of aged books and a hint of Niamh's perfume assaulting his senses. He stood frozen in the entryway, his eyes darting around as if searching for a glimpse of her. The medication from the hospital had dulled the sharp edges of his pain, but the emptiness remained, a gaping void that threatened to swallow him whole.

He shuffled into the living room, each step heavy with the weight of his grief. Memories of Niamh flooded his mind – her laughter echoing through the hallway, the way she'd curl up on the sofa with a book, the scent of her shampoo lingering on the pillows. Jack sank into the couch, his head in his hands as he fought back the tears that threatened to spill over.

He knew he couldn't stay here, surrounded by the ghosts of their past. But where could he go? The funeral home held no appeal, not without Niamh by his side. The thought of facing the sympathetic looks and hushed whispers of the locals made his stomach churn.

He wandered into the kitchen, his eyes landing on the bottle of whiskey that sat on the counter. The temptation to numb the pain was overwhelming, but he knew it would only provide a temporary reprieve. Jack turned away, his gaze falling on the stack of mail that had accumulated in his absence. Bills, condolence cards, and a letter from the police department – a reminder of the reality he now faced.

He moved to their bedroom. The heavy silence contrasted with the storm raging within him. Niamh's belongings lay scattered across the floor, each item an echo of her vibrant presence, now absent. With trembling hands, he packed her clothes into cardboard boxes, the bright hues a mockery of his grief.

He picked up her leather jacket, the one she'd been

wearing when they first met. The scent of her perfume, faint but persistent, lingered. He buried his face in the worn leather, the salty sting of tears mixing with the comforting familiarity of her scent. Grief, a monstrous wave, crashed over him, and his shoulders shook with the force of his sobs. His carefully constructed numbness cracked, and the raw ache of loss threatened to consume him.

The grief abruptly twisted into a surge of hot rage. He flung the jacket down, knocking the half-packed boxes to the floor. They lay there, pathetic and incomplete, just like him. With a growl of frustration, he grabbed a box and yanked the contents out, spilling them across the room.

His movements were frenzied as he attempted to fill the vacuum within. He stormed into his office, the clutter like a physical manifestation of the chaos in his mind. He dumped the box on his desk with no regard for ceremony and filled it with a selection of rare books worn with years of careful use. Finally, after a moment's hesitation, he placed the ancient grimoire on top.

———

The vintage hearse rumbled to life, the throaty engine a defiant roar against the silence. With grim resolve, Jack guided the vehicle onto the road, leaving a swirling cloud of dust in its wake.

He pulled the hearse to the curb outside the funeral home gate and retrieved a heavy padlock and chain from the back of the vehicle. The box of rare books sat there, almost accusingly, but he ignored them.

With swift, methodical movements, he wrapped the rusted chain around the wrought iron bars of the gate; the links clanging like manacles. The padlock snapped shut with a final click, sealing off the past.

For a moment, he stood, fingers clenched around the cool

metal. Then he pulled the keys from his pocket and separated the worn, familiar hearse key from the rest. Anger boiled up again, a last, fiery surge of emotion before he extinguished it. The keyring, with its reminders of the life taken from him, disappeared into the tangle of trees across the road with a final, cathartic fling.

There was no going back. Not to the business, not to the cottage, not to the broken shell of the man he had become.

He slammed the hearse door shut and fired up the engine. The old beast responded with a growl, ready to carry him toward whatever horrors the future held.

CHAPTER 14
BOOKSELLER

The back alley buzzed with a grimy energy, a hidden world away from prying eyes. Overflowing bins spewed their contents and crumpled papers skittered across the cracked pavement. Parked among the shadows was Jack's vintage hearse, its once gleaming chrome now crusted with a layer of city filth.

Two boys, fuelled by mischief, crept closer to the vehicle. One, younger with a mop of tangled hair, darted forward, wiping a circle of dirt from the window and peered inside, face pressed against the glass. The older boy, emboldened, slapped the hearse with a gleeful shout. "Yah! Yah!"

A muffled *SLAM* came from within the hearse. Before they could react, a voice harsh with disuse bellowed out, "Ouch! Little fuckers!"

The children shrieked, legs pumping as they fled the alley, their laughter echoing off crumbling brick walls. They disappeared around a corner, leaving only a fading trace of adrenaline-fuelled giggles.

The rear doors of the hearse flew open, and Jack tumbled out. His once crisp suit was crumpled and stained, his beard wild and untamed. He blinked against the meager light filtering into the alley, eyes narrowed in a scowl. Though his stance was braced for a fight, the only enemy was his own disorientation.

"Little bastards," he muttered.

With weary steps, he returned to the hearse to survey the aftermath of the night before. The back of the hearse contained a threadbare sleeping bag, a few battered boxes... and the scattered remnants of his search for solace at the bottom of a bottle. He snatched up an empty can, the rattle a mournful echo in the alley's stifling silence. A flicker of regret crossed his face before he steeled himself, crushing the can against the brick wall. Two trips with the remaining cans and bottles and the overflowing bins absorbed his discarded attempts at oblivion.

Back at the hearse, Jack pulled out his worn wallet, the emptiness mocking him. "Jaysus." He thought he was good for cash for the rest of the week. Leaning into the back, he found the battered box that held the grimoire and his diminished collection of antique books. "Who's up today?"

A part of him knew that conversing with a box filled with books was not a socially accepted norm. The same part scolded him for neglecting his medication and failing to visit the doctor he had promised to see after being discharged from the hospital. But the only conversation he had these days, if he was being honest, was this one.

His hand hovered over the grimoire for a lingering moment, then he rummaged around and selected some of the others before he shoved the box back into its hiding spot.

With one last glance at the depressing alley, Jack slid into the driver's seat. The engine roared to life, and he pulled out, leaving whatever ghosts were there behind him.

———

The faded sign for *Boyle's Antiquarian Books & Curios* hung over a grimy shop window which almost obscured the shop's interior. This ramshackle haven was a far cry from the polished auction houses where Jack used to do business. But he wasn't an undertaker anymore, just a desperate man trying to slowly kill himself.

A tinkle of the old-fashioned bell announced his entrance into the cramped and dusty shop. Jack weaved through the labyrinth of haphazardly stacked books and cluttered shelves, the air thick with the scent of decaying paper and forgotten time.

Behind the cluttered counter, Martin Boyle hunched over a hefty volume, his pinched face the picture of miserly concentration. Even as Jack set the stack of books down, Boyle refused to acknowledge him.

"Martin." The single word cut through the stale air, a demand rather than a greeting.

Boyle's only response was a cursory glance at the pile, his lip curling into a sneer. "Jack. To what do I owe the pleasure?"

"I thought you might be interested in these." Jack's voice held a forced casualness he didn't feel. These books were his last sliver of respectability, the connection to the life he once knew. A small piece of him died each time he sold one.

Boyle heaved a theatrical sigh and finally tore his gaze from the tome. "Eighty euros."

"Oh, come on! They'd fetch ten times that at auction." Jack knew it was a bluff. He wouldn't survive until any auction, not without funds.

Boyle arched a thin eyebrow. He turned his head as his beady eyes roamed over the cluttered shelves. "Funny," he said. "I don't see any other bidders."

The sting of defeat washed over Jack. He was cornered, desperate... and Boyle knew it. "I'll take it," he muttered, the words bitter in his mouth.

Boyle cracked open the ancient till, the clatter of change painful to Jack's ears, and counted out the amount agreed.

Jack snatched the meager notes, his fingers trembling with a mix of anger and humiliation.

As he turned to leave, Boyle's thin voice pierced the silence. "Jack."

Jack paused, a scowl carved onto his face as he glared back at the shopkeeper.

"My offer is still open. Five hundred euros for the grimoire." Boyle licked his lips, a predatory gleam in his eye. "If you still have it, that is."

"Fuck off," Jack said, the word laced with disgust. He slammed the shop door behind him, the echo rattling in the dusty quiet.

CHAPTER 15
SHOPPING

The fluorescent lights of the supermarket buzzed and flickered, a harsh glare that did little to dispel the bleakness gnawing at Jack. He walked down the alcohol aisle, footsteps echoing in the early morning empty aisles. Each judgmental glance from passing shoppers cut into his already battered dignity, each whisper a reminder of his fall from grace.

The security guard lurked at the end of the aisle, his suspicious gaze a constant, irritating presence. Jack squared his shoulders, a defiant swagger masking the hollowness within. He was a creature of habit, even in his descent into oblivion.

He grabbed two bottles of the cheapest whiskey, their weight a promise in his shaking hands. The clink against the vodka already in his basket sent a thread of anticipation through him. His stomach churned, a mix of nausea and urgent need. Maybe a few bottles of wine to soften the hard edges, then a six-pack for the inevitable comedown. It was barely enough, but it would have to do.

A young mum, nose wrinkled in disgust, hurried past him, nearly stumbling over her own child. He tipped his hat to her. "Ma'am."

The woman scurried away, clutching her child tighter. He watched her retreat, a twisted smirk tugging at the corner of his mouth. Once, he might have blushed at that look of horrified pity. Now, it was just another stone he was building his wall of isolation with, another barrier between him and a world that no longer had a use for him. His drink-laden basket became a badge of pride. They could stare, they could whisper... in fact, it was preferable instead of them trying to help. He was beyond their sympathy, a ghost trapped in a world he no longer belonged in.

At the checkout, the cashier's monotone barely registered as the prices flashed on the screen. "Have you got a club card?"

His hand shook violently as he fished out the crumpled bills, heart pounding. Had she noticed? The sweat prickled his skin from the shame and desperation within. "Sorry. Must have left it at home."

He shoved the bottles into his worn bags, their bulk a comforting pressure against his side. Beyond caring about their judgment, he craved those drinks and the blessed oblivion they provided. He was out of place here, amidst the normalcy and bright lights.

"Seventy-two fifty," said the cashier.

He handed over the notes he'd only recently received from Martin, and the cashier handed him back some coins.

Soon, in the blessed dimness of his hearse, the accusing eyes and the relentless headache would blur into nothingness. For a little while, just a little while, nothing else would matter.

He looked down at his meager change. Food first, though.

———

The scent of greasy burgers and stale fries assaulted Jack's nose like a swarm of aggressive flies. Not that he minded. The familiar salt and fat in the bland flavours brought comfort.

He fell into place at the end of the short queue, eyeing the menu board with only mild interest. It hadn't changed in years - the same cheap, generic fare that filled a hole and not much else.

"Next." The cashier's voice was bored, an almost robotic monotone.

"Hi. Can I get four hamburgers from the eurosaviour menu?" He didn't bother to keep the wryness from his tone.

The cashier's fingers danced across the register with practiced efficiency. "Four euros."

Jack fished coins from his pocket, counting them out. The small pile clinked as they hit the plastic tray.

After a few minutes, Jack strolled out, his footsteps echoing in the near-deserted restaurant. Outside, he rummaged in the brown paper bag. Burgers went into pockets – two on the sides of his jacket, one tucked into the inner breast pocket. The paper bag went into a nearby bin as he chomped into the remaining burger, savouring the blandness, the absence of any real flavour. The street was bustling with midday foot traffic, but he moved counter to the flow, a solitary figure against the human tide.

CHAPTER 16
GRAVEROBBER

The hearse stank of sweat, cheap beer, and the lingering ghosts of those it had once carried. Jack didn't mind. At least the view of the cemetery was decent. Through bleary eyes, he watched the funeral across the overgrown field. Figures clustered around a dark hole in the earth, a priest droning out the same old prayers.

He took a swig of the lukewarm beer, grimacing at the metallic aftertaste, then unwrapped a half-squashed burger from his greasy hoard. Funerals always stirred up an appetite, a morbid sort of hunger. *Should've set up a mobile takeaway*, he thought with a twist of his mouth that might have been a grin. Hot dogs, burgers... a proper feast for the mourners. Jack Cullinan's All-You-Can-Eat Grief Buffet.

The absurdity of it made him chuckle. He tipped his head back, draining the can. Somewhere, far back in the fog of his mind, a disapproving voice whispered about respect and decorum. He crushed the can underfoot, and its small protest barely cut through his haze of self-loathing and half-numb misery.

Back when he'd been a funeral director, he used to find a strange fascination in funerals – the final public performance of a life. The focus of his interest was on the families. The masks of sorrow, sometimes thin and wavering, sometimes so meticulously constructed they fooled even the person wearing them. Jack had always prided himself on seeing beyond those masks.

Guilt gnawed at his insides as sharp as any hunger. *That fucking book!* He couldn't help but think that if he'd remembered it, none of this would've happened. Those things never would have got their claws into Niamh, never would have torn her away, leaving his world a barren wasteland. That was on him, his failure to protect her.

He looked down at the burger, but the want of it had left him. After rewrapping it, he quickly stuffed it back into his pocket. He took another drink of lukewarm beer instead.

———

Sleep hadn't brought rest, only nightmares that clawed and swirled like smoke. His waking was a panicked jolt against the confines of the hearse, the stink of stale beer sour in his nostrils. Empty cans rattled as he scrambled for balance, his heart pounding in his hungover skull.

Jack blinked, his eyes adjusting to the dim light filtering through the hearse's windows. A sharp tug at his jacket pocket jolted him fully awake. He looked down to see a scrawny fox, its russet fur matted and dull, attempting to pull something from his pocket.

"Gwann to fuck!" Jack swatted at the fox, but it remained undeterred, its jaws clamped firmly on the fabric.

With a snarl, the fox gave a vicious yank, and Jack realised what it was after: the last burger, now a misshapen lump in his pocket.

Jack stumbled out, the uneven ground doing little to improve his swaying equilibrium. The fox, a flicker of tawny fur in the moonlight, vanished over the old stone wall.

"Fuck," he muttered again, blinking hard to shake the sleep-grit from his eyes. The moon caught his full attention – swollen, heavy in the night sky, its pale light turning the weathered stones into spectral presences. He'd been hoping for clouds, but what could he do?

The crowbar was an old friend, a tool of the trade tucked away with the spare tire and the half-empty bottles. It was almost comforting, the familiar weight of it in his hand. He hopped the wall with unexpected agility, landing on the earth softened by recent rain.

He dashed, first crossing the field, then weaving between the rows of familiar headstones. The air was still, the silence a heavy blanket broken only by the soft crunch of his footsteps on the path.

———

The Mulvaney tomb loomed ahead of him, a blocky shadow against the gentler curves of older headstones. Margaret Mulvaney had been a formidable old woman - rich, sharp as a tack, and not the sort for quiet funerals. This mausoleum was a statement, a final declaration of the family's status even in death.

Just perfect, thought Jack as he forced open the mausoleum door with his crowbar. He winced at the CRACK that sounded out when the lock gave. It sounded loud as a gunshot, so he hurriedly entered, easing the door closed behind him.

Inside, the air was close, thick with the dry scent of dust and stale chrysanthemums left on a long-forgotten birthday. His footsteps resounded as he flicked on his pocket torch. The beam cut through the gloom, bouncing off polished brass plaques commemorating generations of Mulvaneys.

"There you are." His voice sounded scratchy in the silence.

The plaque was near the floor, the name engraved in neat letters:

Here Lies Margaret Mulvaney.
Loving Mother and Grandmother.
R.I.P.

A flicker of amusement twisted Jack's mouth. Margaret Mulvaney had, in life, been neither loving nor grandmotherly. Respect for the dead was ingrained deep, but respect didn't extend to hypocritical epitaphs.

The crowbar made quick work of the wall covering. The coffin slid out with a muted groan of wood on stone. Jack bent over, readying himself, then stilled.

A sniff. A soft whine. Then a sharp, insistent bark from outside.

He whirled, heart pounding a frantic tattoo. Footsteps crunched on gravel, getting closer. A voice, gruff and questioning, "What is it, boy?"

Jack dived for the door, slamming it shut, his hands fumbling for the handles. Dark shapes pressed against the stained glass above: a canine silhouette and a deeper blur that had to be a man.

The handle rattled with a force that made Jack's teeth jar. He gritted his teeth, straining to hold it shut, sweat stinging his eyes.

"Nothin' here. Come on, boy."

The retreating voice was heaven-sent, but Jack stayed frozen, counting under his breath until he dared to move.

Then he was back at the casket, his fingers working numbly. When he opened the coffin, Margaret Mulvaney lay in eternal repose; her leathery skin stretched taut over her face, her eyes closed. Yet, even in death, her stern disapproval permeated the confined space of the casket, her silent judgment echoing in Jack's ears. He could almost hear her scornful whispers, a haunting symphony that added to his mounting anxiety.

"Margaret. Looking well." It was the only apology he could manage.

The necklace yielded with an unsettling ease, its golden gleam dancing mockingly in the harsh, unforgiving torchlight. The matching earrings followed suit, each requiring a delicate twist before they, too, disappeared into the recesses of his pocket. He executed the act with such swiftness that it seemed to resonate with Margaret's stern disapproval, further intensifying the weight of his guilt in the cold, still air.

"Much obliged." His voice reverberated in the tomb.

He slid the coffin back into place, replacing the covering to mask his handiwork. A final check, his gaze sweeping the small interior, the gleam of metal, the undisturbed dust. He was out the door in seconds, the crowbar tucked under his arm, his movements driven by a desperate, hunted sort of urgency.

———

The shadows between headstones twisted and darkened as he scurried through the graveyard, a rat in a maze built for the dead. His approaching hangover didn't help matters.

Moonlight painted the path ahead in a silvery sheen, turning the worn tombstones into ghoulish sentinels. He was almost there, the low stone wall marking the boundary just ahead, then a bark shattered the stillness, echoing off the silent monuments.

"Fuck." It was a prayer more than a curse. He crouched behind a crumbling cherub, its face weathered smooth, and peered back.

The dog was gaining, snarls tearing through the night air. It was a big, rangy mutt, the sort bred for guarding more than companionship. The caretaker was a slower shape behind, more a suggestion of a threat than an actual one.

Jack gauged the distance to the wall. No chance of making it in a clean dash. Damn dog was too fast, its eyes fixed on its quarry in that single-minded canine way.

He tugged off his jacket, ignoring the chill that bit into his arms. There was only one option left. Risky, maybe, but anything was better than getting cornered and having to explain himself to an irate caretaker.

The jacket went over his arm, thick layers of worn cloth bunching against his skin. He turned, facing the dog, raising the makeshift shield. He had enough cop-on to know the basics: protect your face, present a larger target, hope like hell the other guy – or in this case, beast – got tired first.

He had the crowbar in his other hand. The dog bared down, all teeth and hair and speed. It launched at Jack, a dark blur. Jack caught the savage bite on his covered arm and brought the crowbar down in a sharp *WHACK* to the dog's head.

"Leave 'im, you bastard," shouted the caretaker. He wasn't far away.

Jack whacked the dog once, twice more. It released its bite, but the jacket went with it. With no time to spare to retrieve his jacket, Jack was off, over the boundary wall, and legging it across the field for his hearse.

CHAPTER 17
BIRTH

The cry burst from Niamh's throat. "Fuck! Fuck! Fuck! Jaaaack!" Each repetition was a prayer, a curse, and a plea all at once.

Pain ripped through her. Not the sharp, localised sting of a wound, but the deep, primitive kind that threatened to tear her apart, to split her body so her spirit could escape. Her hands clawed at the threadbare sheet beneath her, damp with sweat and the slickness of blood.

A shadow moved near her – one of The Sisters, their black robes blurring in her tear-filled vision. The porcelain mask offering neither comfort nor a flicker of concern.

Another wave of agony crashed over Niamh, squeezing a strangled scream from her lungs. The world blurred, narrowed to a single point of fire. Then, with a final, monstrous effort fuelled by a mother's desperate love, it was over.

Silence fell, broken only by her own rasping breaths. The Sister moved, and suddenly there was another sound - a thin, reedy cry. Squalling. Her baby.

"Can I hold her?" Niamh propped herself up on shaky

elbows, the weakness of her body nothing compared to the surging need inside her.

The Sister turned, her gaze passing over Niamh as if she were nothing but a piece of discarded furniture. A circle of black-clad bodies had materialized, surrounding the wailing child as a wall of sharks might encircle a wounded fish.

"She needs me!" Niamh's voice was a frayed thread, barely audible above the baby's cries.

No one looked her way. No one answered. The Sister carrying the baby turned and left the room, the circle closing behind her like a silent, implacable tide.

"I just want to hold her!" The words were choked with sobs now. Niamh collapsed back against the rough bed, the tears coming hot and fast. This place, these bitches... they were not simply cruel, they were inhuman. They'd ripped her away from her husband and now took her child, with all the detachment of surgeons removing a cancerous tumor.

Through her anguish, a cold terror began to coil around her heart. Jack... where was he? What had they done to Jack?

———

Rain drummed a tinny rhythm on the roof of the hearse, a dreary backdrop to the dreams curling around the edges of Jack's consciousness. The dreams smelled like stale beer and rot, and had the gnawing, guilt-soaked texture of despair.

Somewhere out there, it was morning. It was a world of alarm clocks and coffee mugs, of people on their way to jobs and routines. A world he no longer belonged to.

The rumble of an engine cut through the rain like a rusty knife. It grew louder, closer, then the screech of brakes interrupted it, followed by a series of beeps. A bin lorry, reversing into the alley with the ungainly grace of an elephant in a china shop.

Two figures spilled out from the cab, their orange waterproof gear gleaming almost garishly against the grimy brick walls. They went about their job with practiced efficiency, the metallic clang of bins echoing with a violence that ripped through whatever haze still clung to Jack's brain.

Jack opened the back door of the hearse and peered out. "What the hell, lads?" he rasped. His head pounded a counterpoint to the bin-induced racket.

"Take it up with your landlord, eh?" The younger of the binmen grinned, showing teeth that needed a good brushing.

His mate let out a guffaw, the sound bouncing off the damp brick and drilling into Jack's skull.

There was no point arguing, no point in explaining, even if the words would form right. He just wanted his blessed silence back, the cocoon of his miserable solitude.

Rolling over with a groan, Jack slammed the back doors of the hearse shut. Inside, everything was mercifully muffled. He tugged his sleeping bag over his head to blot out the relentless clatter of a city waking up without him.

Sleep came on little cat feet, easing some of the tension in his throbbing head. It wouldn't last, but it was enough to drown out the echoes of a world that no longer had space for him.

———

Jack's heart pounded a frantic drumbeat against his ribs as he ran. The hallway twisted before him, its panelling warped into a hideous mockery of itself. Portraits leered, their eyes like pits, and the once stately statues in their niches writhed and shifted, their stone faces contorted. The air throbbed with an unseen menace, and every shadow twitched with a life of its own. Where the hell is this?

Ahead, Niamh shimmered into view, her white dress a beacon in the suffocating gloom. "Bring it to me, Jack," she pleaded, her voice a thin thread against the growing pulse of fear.

He looked down. The grimoire cradled in his arms felt wrong —

rough wood against his skin, a weight that dragged at him even as he ran. Panic flared in his gut. "Niamh!"

"Run! Don't let go!" As the hallway narrowed around them, Jack saw her vanishing into the next twisted corridor.

"Niamh?" His voice cracked. The sense of something wrong, something pursuing him, clawed at his spine. A glance over his shoulder revealed his fear made real.

The nun glided after him with unnatural speed, her porcelain face blank, her eyes like dark sockets with glowing pinpoints dead centre. The black fabric of her habit billowed with a wind that didn't exist, whipping and coiling like snakes.

Niamh screamed, a sound that cut through him colder than any blade. "Run, my love!" He didn't have to be told twice. Legs burning, lungs aching, he sprinted after his wife, slamming into walls as the corridors narrowed, turning, twisting into endless, impossible angles. Yet Niamh remained just out of reach, her spectral form a flickering promise.

"Don't let her go, Jack! Hold on to her!"

Breath rasping in his throat, he risked a glance down. The grimoire was gone. In its place, a bundle wrapped in swaddling linen filled his arms.

Niamh's scream pierced the air, a keening cry of terror. He spun, and the nun was upon him, reaching out with impossible swiftness. She tore the bundle from his grasp, and a blow of unseen force sent him hurtling backward.

"Noooo!" Niamh's voice faded even as he scrambled up, launching himself at the retreating nun, fists flailing. The black cloth of her habit fought him, pushing him back, smothering him.

Then came the silence, the suffocating, crushing silence that was more terrifying than any scream.

CHAPTER 18
USED BOOKS

Jack woke with a gasp, thrashing about, the sleeping bag twisted around him, a suffocating shroud amplifying his panic. Clawing his way free, he flailed about, hands scrabbling in search of the bundle. In search of his child.

Reality slammed into him with the force of a headstone. He was in the hearse, the stale air heavy with the scent of his own misery. The dream lingered at the edges of his memory, its terror fading from a howl to an insistent, gnawing ache.

His gaze darted around, seeking the warm comfort of a bottle, the blessed chemical oblivion he craved. Empty cans mocked him. A few stray drops gleamed in the hollow of a discarded bottle. Not enough. Never enough.

With a tremor that ran through his entire body, he turned away, forcing his shaking hands to crawl over to the battered cardboard box. His collection, once his pride and joy, was now a graveyard of sold dreams. The grimoire lay there, its worn cover seeming to pulse in the half-light. The only valuable item left.

"No." The word was a croak, barely more than a whisper.

He slammed the lid back down, shoving the box away as if it could burn him.

"Not that one. It can't be that one."

He sat rocking, squeezing his eyes shut to blot out the image of Niamh's terror-filled eyes, of the nun with her empty gaze and her grasping hands. He picked up another empty bottle, trying to find a last elusive drop in its depths. Nothing.

With a violence born of desperation, he hurled the bottle away. It shattered against the inside of the hearse, the sound echoing the fracturing inside his own mind.

"Fuck it." The decision clawed its way up from a place where reason had long taken leave.

Grabbing the box, he ripped it open, hands tearing at the cardboard. The grimoire was there, an island of ancient knowledge in a sea of wreckage. The touch of it was like ice on his skin.

Tucking the book under his arm, he climbed out of the hearse, his legs unsteady, his resolve a fragile thing.

———

Jack marched across the dusty floor of Boyle's bookshop, the grimoire clutched under his arm like a stolen treasure or a ticking time bomb. He slammed it onto the counter with a force that made Martin Boyle jump. The man's eyes widened, then greed shimmered beneath the surface of his nervous frown.

"Don't start, Martin." The words crackled with the edge of Jack's despair. He wasn't in the mood for the haggling, the wheedling, the pretense that this was just another dusty old book.

Boyle licked his lips, eyes glued to the grimoire. "Right you are, Jack." His voice carried surprise and a touch of respect.

"You said five hundred euros." Jack leaned over the

counter. Part of him, some ragged scrap of sanity, balked at this, but he shoved it down. There was no time for guilt or hesitation.

"Well, it's been a slow-" Boyle began, then saw the hard set of Jack's jaw. Perhaps he knew a desperate man when he saw one.

"You can have it for six."

Boyle didn't argue, just opened the till and counted out the notes, trying to appear nonchalant, failing miserably. He laid the cash alongside the grimoire, then produced a register receipt that was more formality than necessity.

Jack hesitated. His fingers twitched toward the book, that link to the world where Niamh was by his side. But the sight of the cash, the promise of enough money to drown the night-mares, at least for a little while... it was too strong a pull.

Before he could reconsider, before his tattered morality could find its voice again, he snatched up the cash and receipt.

Boyle moved with surprising swiftness, grabbing the grimoire and disappearing with it beneath the counter. "Thanks for the business, Jack, but I'm afraid I'm closing early today."

It wasn't a suggestion to leave, it was a command. Jack's fingers curled into fists. This was wrong, every inch of it. But at least he had the cash to go out in style. He turned away, pocketed the notes and receipt, and allowed Martin to hustle him out into the street.

———

Martin closed the shop door and locked it, breathing a sigh of relief. He carried *The Book of Ravens* into his back office, his heart racing with anticipation. Setting it down on his desk, he stared at the ancient tome, hardly daring to touch it.

The leather binding had become worn and cracked, the

pages yellowed with age. Strange symbols adorned the cover, their meaning lost to time. Martin knew it was a rare piece.

"Ah, you beauty," he whispered, letting his fingers caress the worn leather. He could almost feel the centuries of power humming beneath his fingertips. *The Book of Ravens* was more than a rare piece; it was a legend, whispered about in hushed tones among those who knew such things.

With trembling hands, he opened the book, the musty smell of old parchment filling his nostrils. Intricate illustrations and cryptic text filled the pages, written in a language he couldn't decipher. He traced his fingers over the faded ink, marvelling at the craftsmanship.

Martin felt a sense of satisfaction knowing he'd rescued the book. He shook his head at the thought of Jack Cullinan having possession of such a treasure. "Ignorant feckin' waster," he muttered. The man had no clue what he'd possessed, too lost in his own misery to appreciate the grimoire's true value.

Leaning back in his chair, Martin allowed himself a small smile. He'd have to be careful who he showed this to, but he knew the right collector would pay a fortune for such a rare find. If he didn't keep it for himself, that was.

CHAPTER 19
SUPPLIES

Niamh surfaced out of the depths of despair-laden sleep like a diver coming up for air too quickly. Her eyelids felt glued shut, her body sluggish and heavy. Someone was shaking her, a hand insistent on her shoulder.

"Where's my baby?" Her voice was thick, barely a whisper that snagged on the edges of her raw throat.

The figure beside her shifted. A woman crisp and severe, in a tailored suit that looked out of place in the room. No nun's robes, but the same chill hardness in her eyes.

"Get dressed," the woman said. Her tone held no warmth, no hint of sympathy. "You'll see her soon."

A tracksuit was thrust into Niamh's hands - clean, new, a parody of comfort in this place. A flicker of anger sparked in her. Where was Jack? Where was the Sister who'd haunted her dreams?

But the crushing weight of exhaustion dragged her down, and the promise – "You'll see her soon." – was a lifeline she clung to with her remaining strength. Her daughter. She'd endured the ordeal of birth, the wrenching separation... for the chance to simply see her child again? A flicker of something like hope fought its way past the grief and terror.

Her body moved on autopilot. The tracksuit rasped against her skin as she pulled it on, the rough fabric a contrast to the soft swaddling she'd last seen her baby wrapped in. She wanted to scream, to rage, but even that fire felt banked. Her only strength left was this single-minded focus: to get to her baby.

Straightening, Niamh faced the woman, her chin lifted in a defiance too weak to show in her voice. "Now?"

If the woman noticed the tremor that ran through Niamh's body, she gave no sign. The response was a brief nod and a pointing motion toward the door. *One step at a time*, Niamh thought, pushing back the memories that threatened to drown her. One step at a time, and somewhere, maybe, her child waited.

———

Jack drifted through the supermarket alcohol aisle like a ghost, the bright fluorescent lights highlighting his gaunt face and bloodshot eyes. His fingers twitched toward the familiar rows of cheap vodka, the plastic bottles promising blessed oblivion at a bargain price.

But something made him pause. *Why the hell not?* The thought came unbidden, a dark whisper that echoed in the back of his head. He'd fallen too far, lost too much to care about the finer things... usually. But now, with the grimoire sold, with the cash burning a hole in his pocket, he would make a grand gesture.

His hand moved, not to the usual rotgut, but to a shelf a notch above. The labels here gleamed with names instead of just types. There was even a dusty bottle of something French he couldn't pronounce. He picked up a bottle, hefting it experimentally. The weight felt good in his hand, the smooth glass more solid than the cheap plastic he was used to.

"Yes. Why the hell not?" he muttered to himself. The words bounced off the shelves, a strange sort of mockery in this ordinary place.

At the checkout, the cashier, the same woman from his humiliating encounter days, weeks ago - how long had it been? – raised a delicately plucked eyebrow.

"Special occasion?"

A laugh rumbled in Jack's chest – harsh, too loud. "I'll make my last drink a good one."

The cashier's eyebrows threatened to disappear into her hairline.

"Giving it up?"

Jack shrugged, the movement dislodging a shower of stale breadcrumbs from his jacket. "Something like that." As if any of it mattered now. The cashier's silence was a judgment, but he couldn't bring himself to care. It was all the same in the end: fancy liquor or the stuff that cleaned paintbrushes; it all led to the same oblivion.

Jack moved down the hardware store aisle with the resoluteness of a man collecting supplies for a siege. His fingers twitched as he bypassed the hammers and nails, his gaze landing on the coils of rope hanging in neat rows. He picked up a length, feeling the rough texture under his fingers, testing its strength with a sharp tug. Putting it back, he repeated the process, a frown drawing his brows together. Each discarded coil was a decision made, a step closer to a plan taking concrete, terrifying form.

The question hung in the air, unspoken but echoing off the shelves. Would this one hold? Ninety kilos, give or take. *Sturdy enough.*

A flicker of movement caught his eye. A store clerk, a young woman in an orange apron, was passing on her rounds. Jack stepped into her path, the rope held out like an offering.

"Excuse me, I wonder if you can help."

The woman sighed, a flicker of annoyance crossing her face. "Of course, sir."

"Would you say this would bear my weight? Say, ninety kilos?" He knew he must look a sight. Unshaven, unwashed, despair clinging to his clothes like a stubborn stain. She glanced at him, then at the rope, her confusion turning to a wary sort of pity.

Jack felt a prickle of embarrassment but pushed it away. "I'm building a swing," he lied. The words tasted bitter on his tongue.

The clerk hesitated, then with a shrug that spoke volumes about her doubt, said, "Sure. If the frame... or tree, or whatever, is sturdy enough."

"Great! Much obliged!" Jack turned away, a lightness in his step that had nothing to do with relief. The rope was the last piece of the puzzle. Now all he had to do was find the right tree.

CHAPTER 20
CHANCE ENCOUNTER

Jack drove on autopilot, the liquor bottles and coil of rope mocking him from the passenger seat. His mind churned, the poisonous blend of alcohol and turbulent emotions pushing aside memories he'd dulled for days.

The traffic light was a red blur against the grey cityscape. He slammed on the brakes; the hearse lurched in protest. Four cars ahead, sleek and black, a luxury car pulled into the left lane.

For a moment, time halted. At the passenger window of the luxury car, a face turned - a blur that resolved into a familiar heart-shaped curve, dark eyes dull and tired, an unforgettable tumble of black curls.

"Niamh?" The name was a choked whisper, a prayer lost in the roar of the traffic.

And then a truck, a lumbering green beast, slid into place between him and that flash of recognition. It obscured his view, breaking the fragile thread of connection like a snapped rope.

"No, no, no!" The words ripped from his throat. Seat belt abandoned, he scrambled out of the hearse, ignoring the blaring horns, the angry shouts of drivers.

The traffic light flickered to green, the truck inched forward... and the black car was gone. He stood helpless on the tarmac, the city a cacophony of noise that mocked the echoing silence inside his head.

Back in the hearse, the weight of the rope pulled his gaze, and his resolve crumbled a little more. The pursuit was reckless, bordering on delusional. He'd seen a woman, a flicker of resemblance. That was all. Yet... a corner of his soul screamed it was her, that Niamh was close, and he had to reach her.

He slammed the hearse into gear, cutting across traffic in a manoeuvre that drew a chorus of outraged horns and rude gestures. "Fuck you," he shouted, but inside he was elated. Jack Cullinan had found his purpose again.

He drove with the ferocity of a man possessed, the city blurring around him in a haze of motion. The blare of car horns faded as he surged after the black car, weaving through traffic with reckless abandon. He hunched over the wheel, eyes narrowed, the liquor in his bloodstream replaced with a raw surge of adrenaline. He might have lost Niamh once, but goddamn if he'd lose her again.

The sleek car stayed just ahead, a beacon in the urban sprawl. He didn't close the distance, knowing better than to alert his quarry to his pursuit. He simply followed, matching its turns and manoeuvres through junctions and roundabouts, his knuckles white on the steering wheel.

Buildings shifted around him as they veered into the older part of town. The grand shops and sleek offices gave way to cracked facades and boarded-up windows. The dwindling traffic made pursuit easier, and soon, nothing separated him from the black car anymore.

It signalled a left turn, and Jack slowed, letting it slip from sight around the corner. Then he pressed the accelerator and rounded the corner himself, satisfaction twisting his lips. The hunt was on.

The familiar ache of despair was a constant in his chest,

but beneath it thrummed an unfamiliar emotion. Hope, maybe. A single desperate, irrational tendril of hope that Niamh was in that car, that this wild chase wasn't just madness, that it was leading him to her.

———

Jack's hearse rolled onto Aranea Street with deceptive calm, the engine grumbling in protest. This was no ordinary street - the cobblestones had been swept clean, the stately Georgian townhouses were gleaming with fresh paint, and even the wrought iron streetlamps had been meticulously restored down to the wisps of cobwebs clinging to their ornamental curves.

The sleek black car sat parked mid-street, an anachronism among the faded grandeur. Jack's heart pounded a panicked tattoo against his ribs. He forced himself to slow, to continue past as if he were an aimless sightseer and not a man on the brink of losing his sanity, maybe even his soul.

As he passed, he risked a glance out of the side window. "Niamh," he whispered, and all doubt vanished. It was her, the curve of her cheek, the defiant tilt of her chin, even slumped in that car seat. Yet, she didn't look up, her gaze seeming to hold a thousand-yard stare. *Dazed, drugged...* the thought clawed at his insides with cold terror.

Jack found a parking space just up the street and settled to watch. His world narrowed to the reflection in his rearview mirror: a smartly dressed driver got out, as did a smartly dressed woman in a grey suit, and Niamh and another woman - young with wild brown hair - were dragged from the car. The driver was rough, but there was no sign of fight left in his wife.

Teeth gritted, Jack switched positions, twisting in his seat to watch out the back window. The driver followed the stylish woman up the steps of one of the townhouses, keeping a firm grip on Niamh and the other woman. A brisk knock, a flash of obscured figures in the doorway, then the door shut behind them.

Jack watched the driver and the woman disappear back into the black car. It pulled out and headed toward him. He ducked, turning away as they passed, and they paid him no mind. A nobody in his battered hearse, not even worth a second glance.

Unnoticed, behind him a fist-sized spider skittered over the hearse's roof. Its eight eyes glittered in the weak sunlight as it moved silently across the weathered metal.

At least Niamh wasn't alone. Whatever place this was, whatever was waiting behind that old door, Niamh faced it in the company of another. And that, maybe, offered the tiniest spark of hope in the darkness Jack found himself lost in.

He slumped back against the seat, the wave of adrenaline receding and leaving in its wake a familiar, crushing exhaustion. The grand plans, the desperate chase, had ended here – a cramped hearse on a deserted street, watching an empty doorway. For a moment, the lure of the liquor was irresistible. Oblivion, blessed silence, it was all he had to dull the sharp edges.

The bottle beckoned, and he gave in. The harsh burn of the spirits was a brutal counterpoint to the hollowness inside him. He took another swig, then smacked his lips with something approaching satisfaction.

The notepad in the glove box was an old habit from funeral planning, and the muscle memory kicked in. He grabbed it and scrawled the street name, the house number, and a crude sketch of the layout as best he could see it. Then, with deliberate movements, he adjusted the rearview mirror, finding the best angle he could for comfortable observation.

He took another sip of liquor and recapped the bottle. He knew it was a fine line. Too much liquor would muddle his thinking, but he needed enough to keep his head straight and the shakes at bay until he had enough information about the situation Niamh was in.

He settled back in the driver's seat. The hearse was his world. The woman in that house was his purpose. He would wait. He would watch. And maybe he would find something - an angle, a pathway forward, a way in. A sliver of hope strong enough to cut through the darkness.

CHAPTER 21
ARANEA STREET

Time bled into itself during Jack's stakeout. Day stretched into a long, hazy twilight, then blurred into a night lit only by the weak glow from the cobweb-shrouded streetlights. He noted each arrival with jerky scrawls on the notepad, his hands tremorous from a mix of alcohol and the tension coiled tight in his gut.

Gentleman With Cane.

Executive Type.

Celebrity Type.

A parade of men, all purposeful, all welcomed inside that forbidding townhouse, painted a picture in shades Jack knew all too well. The Gentleman, his posture too stiff, betrayed a certain eagerness. The Executive, a quick look over his shoulder before disappearing inside. Even the Celebrity, with his limo parked out of sight, had arrived not in a blaze of glory but with the furtive air of a man with something to hide.

Spiders crept and scuttled around the hearse, silent

weavers of suffocating webs. He watched them, the relentless industry mocking his chaotic attempts at observation.

A final frantic scribble, then the realisation hit him with the force of a blow.

"Shit!" The word was a hoarse echo in the hearse's silence. He sank back, gazing at his reflection as though it was a stranger. Dirty, unshaven, eyes red-rimmed and sunken, he looked like the worst desperate punter he'd ever ushered into a hastily arranged viewing.

The notepad was a ragged indictment – timings, notes, and at the bottom, the dawning realisation writ large:

Brothel?

A wave of self-loathing washed over him, mingled with the acid bite of the liquor. It was painfully obvious in hindsight. But this wasn't a normal brothel. No garish lights, no seediness, just the sinister trappings of old money and whispered deals behind a respectable facade.

Niamh was in there. Not as a willing participant, he knew that with every fibre of his being. But she was in there, trapped, used. And he, in his drunken, delusional state, had stumbled onto the scene like a blind man, led by a strand woven from his own despair.

———

Something shifted. It started under the hearse, where the cobblestones were all but hidden beneath a dense, glinting layer of spiderwebs. At first, it was just a tremor, a quiver in the intricate silk that held the hearse in place. Then the sickening *CRUNCH* came, followed by the muffled *POP*, as heavy wheels crushed unseen bodies.

The hearse lurched, straining against its spider-spun

restraints. It moved only a few inches, but in that motion, the webs gave way. They stretched, thinned, and tore, the silvery threads snapping with a sound like a chorus of brittle twigs underfoot.

With every inch it gained, the onslaught intensified. More spiders, scuttling in panicked bursts, met their end under the unyielding tires. The hearse shuddered and ground forward, tearing free of its silken prison.

Jack's hearse pulled out of its parking place and onto the silent road, making its way off Aranea Street.

CHAPTER 22
SCRUBBING UP

Jack approached the funeral home like a thief. The overgrown grounds and the chained gate looked less like home and more like a battlefield long deserted. Climbing the gate was an act of weary defiance, every scrape of metal against stone grating on his nerves.

He scurried across the weed-choked driveway, the crunch of gravel echoing too loudly in the silence, and ducked around the back. The crowbar was a familiar friend these days, its weight an ironic comfort in his hand. The cottage door yielded with a groan and a spray of wood splinters. He shouldered his way inside, the opening barely wide enough for him to squeeze through.

Inside the cottage, the air hung heavy with dust and absence. The pile of unopened mail on the floor marked the slow passage of time. He ignored it, the relentless ticking of the everyday world meaningless to him.

His bedroom was a point of chaos, frozen in time, but it only took moments to find fresh clothing. He threw them on the bed and grabbed his old hold-all.

He moved to the other side of the room, to the half-empty drawers and wardrobe where Niamh's things still lay in neatly folded piles. Her scent clung to the worn fabric. He chose a pair of jeans, sturdy boots, a T-shirt, and finally, the leather jacket she went nowhere without.

The items went into the hold-all. She'd need them when he got her out of the brothel. *I'll free her or die trying.* He wasn't leaving Niamh in that place a moment longer than necessary.

––––––

Jack moved to the bathroom, a small oasis in this house of neglect. He shed his filthy clothing with relief. They were in terrible shape, only fit for burning, but he hadn't time for that.

Before turning on the shower, a quick prayer escaped his lips. The water sputtered, choked, then flowed clear and surprisingly warm. Inside the hazy cubicle, he scrubbed at his skin with a viciousness that bordered on self-flagellation. The grime gave way begrudgingly, revealing the pale, hollowed face beneath. His beard and hair got the same treatment, soap stinging his eyes as he worked it into a lather.

He emerged towelling himself dry, the harsh bathroom light unforgiving as he turned to the mirror. The straight razor, a relic of a time when appearances mattered, beckoned from the countertop. He picked it up, noting the weight of it. Months had passed since he'd last used it, but he still remembered the sensation of steel against his skin.

The transformation was brutal. The beard came off in chunks, leaving scrapes that bled pinpricks of crimson on his cheeks. His face emerged from the unruly growth older, gaunt, marked with lines his drinking and pain had cut too deep. It wasn't the face of the Jack Cullinan he knew. "You'll have to do," he muttered to his reflection.

Dressed in clean clothes, a spritz of cologne that smelled of happier times, he picked up the hold-all, then paused. The bathroom door was ajar, a glint of metal catching his eye. He turned back, stepping across the linoleum.

The razor, wiped clean now, felt dangerous in his hand. He tested the blade against his thumb, feeling the sharpness bite.

"You never know," he whispered. Folding it carefully, he slipped it into his back pocket. Maybe it wouldn't come to that. Maybe he could find Niamh, break through the walls of that house, and bring her home.

Maybe.

And if not... well, even a cornered rat would fight. He'd always been the soft one, the gentle one. That Jack Cullinan was dead, but something harder, something with a dangerous edge, remained. There were worse ways to die than fighting for the only thing that still mattered.

CHAPTER 23
THE HOUSE OF MARIONETTES

Jack parked the hearse a careful distance away, the rumble of the idling engine unnatural in the street's stillness. The urge to charge in, to tear that townhouse door down with his bare hands, was overwhelming. Yet, a scrap of practical logic prevailed. If his suspicion was confirmed and the business operating within was a brothel, then it was not a legitimate business, legally speaking. That sort of reckless attack on a criminal enterprise was a death wish, and Niamh needed him alive. He couldn't risk calling the police either, because who knew what connections were involved with keeping such an establishment running? He could only trust himself in freeing his wife, and he would do whatever it took.

A flicker of movement, a gleam of polished steel. The straight razor slid from his pocket into his hand and from there into the side of his shoe. Not elegant, but he didn't intend it for a duel. It was a last-ditch weapon, a taste of the ruthlessness he had to find within himself to survive.

Stepping out of the hearse, he took a deep breath, the air tasting of damp cobblestones and the faint scent of earthy decay. With each step along Aranea Street, his resolve hardened further. This wasn't just a rescue mission anymore. It represented payback, righteous fury, and the desperate gamble of a man who had lost everything but now had a slim chance of recovering it. If he was willing to fight.

He quickened his pace and turned onto Aranea Street, muttering, "Bring it on."

The stained glass above the door proclaimed *The House of Marionettes*. The abstract depictions of string puppets somehow spoke of a playground for the twisted and wealthy, a world where fantasy, perversion, and power intertwined. Terror slithered down Jack's spine, but he quashed it.

He knocked on the door in what he hoped was a confident manner and blurted out his prepared line before the door had opened fully, "Em," he forced the words out, "I'm here for the marionettes?" The lie tasted sour on his tongue. *There's no way he'll buy this*, thought Jack.

The bouncer was a mountain of muscle topped with a face an unkind god had sculpted from leftover clay. He looked Jack up and down. Clearly, this wasn't his usual clientele.

Yet, the door swung open. "In ye go," the man said, his voice a rumble of suspicion. Jack stepped across the threshold and tried not to breathe too deeply. The air in the house was heavy, tainted with something rotten and sweet beyond the expensive decor.

"Far enough," said the bouncer, a massive hand landing on Jack's shoulder. With a frightening display of efficiency, the bouncer patted him down, his fingers probing and insistent. Jack forced himself to relax, to play the wide-eyed customer, while his gaze took in his surroundings.

The hallway, with its tasteful furnishings and antique lamps, could have been in any wealthy home. Except for the cobwebs. Thick, glistening strands were everywhere, stretching from the ceiling to drape over the furniture. Small black shapes scuttled in the periphery of his vision.

"Maid's day off?" asked Jack, keeping his voice light.

A noncommittal grunt from the man as he finished his search. "First time?"

"Here? Yes." Jack knew his best chance lay in playing the naïve newcomer rather than drawing attention with bold claims of experience.

The bouncer pointed toward an open door on the left. "Ye'll be needin' a drink."

Jack pivoted toward the door, but the man's hand shot out, seizing his shoulder in a blatant warning. "No messin' about," he growled.

The sheer power in the man's grasp was staggering, and any retort withered on Jack's tongue. He dipped his head, praying it would suffice, and the giant appeared content. Fingers unclenching, the man granted Jack leave to enter.

———

Stepping into the lounge, Jack felt transported to a bygone era of opulence and indulgence. The tasteful decor was designed to lull a man into a sense of wealth and security, but the ubiquitous cobwebs whispered a darker truth. The bar gleamed in the corner, fully stocked and presided over by a sharply dressed barman. An upright piano added a touch of old-school class to the place.

"The manager will be with you in a moment, sir," the barman said, his voice smooth and practiced. "Can I get you anything while you wait?"

"Whiskey. Neat." Jack perched at the bar wondering if 'the manager' was the name for pimp hereabouts. Was pimp the right word? He had no idea. Before he knew it, he cradled an expensive glass containing an amber liquid. It was excellent quality, no surprise there, and he savoured the first sip.

A flicker of movement, and the manager stepped into the room.

The man entered the room, his confidence obvious in every step. His brown hair, styled in a way that recalled an age a century past, framed a face that was pale with a hint of greenish hue that Jack couldn't quite attribute to the lighting alone. The cut of his 1920s dress suit was flawless, as if he had been plucked from a different era entirely.

Despite his vintage appearance, there was an undeniable air of authority and danger that surrounded him, hinting at the depth of his experience and the secrets he guarded closely. As he moved across the room, his gait was fluid and graceful, possessing an almost otherworldly quality.

He was a man who gave the impression of having lived through countless years, his presence commanding attention and respect. His agelessness was apparent, even as his face bore the marks of time. In his eyes, one could glimpse a life that extended far beyond the realm of ordinary human experience.

"Good evening." The man's eyes flicked over Jack, part appraisal, part curiosity.

"Mister–" Jack began, but the man cut him off.

"Please, Tommy will be fine." His smile was the kind that held promises and threats in equal measure. "Cassius, my doorman, mentioned it's your first time." A quirk of an eyebrow. "How did you hear about us?"

"Oh, well, I promised I wouldn't divulge their name." Jack tried for nonchalance, but there was no hiding his desperation. Trustworthy, reliable, just the sort of man they could manipulate and destroy. Perfect cover.

"Ah. Discreet and loyal. Rare traits indeed." Tommy studied him, making him squirm. "Are you looking for anything in particular?"

"Em, someone... exotic." The words felt wrong on his tongue, like an insult to Niamh, but he couldn't be too specific or he'd give the game away. He'd never been one for brothels either, not even in his youth, but he hoped the inexperience would reinforce his pretense.

"Rest assured, all of our little marionettes are exotic, but I have just the one." Tommy's eyes gleamed with a predatory light. "Cash, I presume?"

Jack fumbled in his pocket, coming up with the crumpled wad of notes from Boyle's. Tommy took them with a nose wrinkle of distaste, then gestured toward the barman. "An attendant will fetch you in a moment."

Jack placed the bills on the bar, not noticing the receipt wrapped within them. When he turned back, Tommy was gone.

Jack relaxed and swallowed the rest of his drink, tapped for another. He'd paid enough for it. The empty was magicked away and a full measure appeared in its place. He settled in to wait.

CHAPTER 24
PREPARATION ROOM

Tommy entered the hidden room in the basement of *The House of Marionettes*, sliding the panel back in place behind him. The dim light cast eerie shadows but was no problem for his eyes. The thick, moist air welcomed him.

Madam Arnott took up most of the room. The French brothel owner transformed entirely over the past hundred years or more. *She is magnificent*, thought Tommy, as he took in her grandeur. Her slim body melded seamlessly with the huge arachnid reproductive system. She was a fusion of human and spider, her skin a pale, translucent hue that glowed in the room, providing its only light. Her eyes, large and black, held a predatory intelligence that followed Tommy's every movement. She awaited him.

"Tommy," she purred, her voice a low, seductive whisper that resonated within his soul. "You know what I require of you."

Tommy nodded, his heart racing with a mixture of fear and desire. He had offered his seed many times before, and he did it eagerly. He adored her and would do anything for her. Coupling with her was supremely pleasurable, not just because the sticky substance exuding from her body was a potent aphrodisiac.

As he approached her, he could feel the heat radiating from her body, a warmth that seeped into his very being. He sensed the power that flowed through her. The brothel and its inhabitants relied on the life force for sustenance.

Slowly, he undressed and placed his neatly folded clothing on a small table by the door. He was fully erect before he was done.

Madam Arnott reached out, her fingers long and spider-like, and caressed Tommy's face. Her touch was icy, yet it sent a wave of pleasure coursing through his body.

"You are mine, Tommy," she whispered, her voice a seductive promise. "And I will reward you for your loyalty."

Tommy's heart swelled with pride and desire. "You're the only reward I need, Madam," he said. He knew that his seed was essential to the brothel's survival, and he felt honoured to offer it. Spidery appendages bent inward from either side and lifted him as though he were a child. They brought him closer to Madam Arnott as she spread herself wide to accept him.

Their bodies pressed together, and Tommy felt the sticky substance that the madam exuded spread over his skin. It sent waves of ecstasy coursing through his body as he entered her. Both of them moaned.

As they coupled, the room pulsed with the energy of their union. The air was thick with the scent of sex and power, and Tommy felt as if he were part of something greater than himself. Indistinct shapes moved in the darkest recesses of the room, but they were no threat to him who spawned them.

Tommy moved faster inside her, feeling light as air held as he was by the madam's limbs. His sweat mingled with her fluids and he bent to kiss her deeply, drinking in her essence as she did his. His loins exploded, and he felt her suck his seed from him.

When she had consumed Tommy's offering, her arachnid limbs lifted him out of her and delicately placed him down on the floor. Madam Arnott smiled, her black eyes filled with gratitude and sated desire.

"Thank you, *mon amour*," she whispered, her voice a low, seductive promise. "Our new children will be with us soon."

Tommy nodded. He could already see movement in the reproductive system surrounding the human part of her.

He dressed quickly, leaving Madam Arnott to the task of spawning. As he left the hidden room, he felt a sense of purpose and belonging, as he always did. He would do anything for the madam, and he looked forward to the next time they would be together.

———

Niamh forced herself to remain still. Stillness was a survival tactic, a way to disappear into the background, her inner self a fortress against the horror closing in around her. The room was stark, its bare furnishings contrasting the emotional storm that consumed the only other person in the room. Dani.

The other woman's sobs grated on Niamh's nerves. Losing control was a luxury she couldn't afford. Every tear, every frantic plea, made Dani a target. Niamh needed to play dead, to fly under the radar, and that meant a steely discipline beyond anything she thought herself capable of.

"What do they want with us?" Dani's voice was a strangled cry. Niamh didn't respond, her gaze a thousand-yard stare aimed just past the other woman. She clung to the cold emptiness; it was her only armour against breaking.

Dani shook her, a desperate attempt to elicit a response. "Say something, for God's sake!"

Then the world shifted. The door opened, and a gentleman strode in, followed by a hulking shadow of a man with leather gloves and a cruel, glinting knife whispering of brutality.

"That one." The man's voice was a whipcrack, his finger pointing at Niamh.

Dani scrambled forward, ignoring the heavy as she prostrated herself at the gentleman's feet. "P-p-p-please, sir! There's been a mistake. I don't belong here!" Sobs choked her voice, her slight frame consumed by terror.

A vicious shove sent Dani sprawling. Something in Niamh tensed, a primal instinct for survival coiling beneath the surface of her feigned helplessness.

"Wait! This one first," said the gentleman, pointing now at Dani.

The henchman switched direction and moved toward Dani instead, then dragged her to the centre of the room like a sacrificial lamb and forced her to her knees. Niamh felt her heart hammer a panicked tattoo against her ribs.

The gentleman moved to the wall and pulled a chain. The sound of gears echoed ominously from above and a trapdoor creaked open, revealing darkness. All eyes locked on the black hole above Dani.

Niamh, to all appearances, remained unseeing. But beneath the facade, her mind raced. With an almost predatory clarity, she analysed her surroundings – the henchman with his back turned, his attention solely on the show in the ceiling, the knife in its sheath.

A scream tore through the air as Dani saw what was crawling through the trapdoor.

———

The scream echoed down the hallway, a thin, piercing sound that clawed at Jack's gut. He turned sharply. "Was that a scream?" Panic threatened to overwhelm his carefully constructed pretense.

The attendant, a severe-faced woman in a shapeless uniform, continued along as if nothing had happened. "You hear all sorts in this place, sir." Her voice was monotone, a dismissal that set Jack further on edge.

Moments later, she unlocked a door and gestured him inside. "I'll be back in an hour, sir." The heavy thud of the door closing behind him echoed in the dimness.

"Em, right you are," he muttered. The words lingered in the silence.

The bedroom crackled with a manufactured sensuality. Pink-tinted light from a single lamp did little to pierce the gloom. A massive four-poster bed swathed in gauzy fabrics dominated the room, and on it, a woman lounged, beckoning him closer as the last echo of the scream faded from his mind.

"Good evening, miss." His voice sounded thin, brittle. Even in this den of forced intimacy, a prickle of unease crawled across his skin.

She beckoned again, her movements languid, yet somehow wrong.

"Em. I'm looking for someone. Maybe you can help?" His hands rose in a placating gesture, his act of an eager client unravelling.

Her response was a slow, seductive grind of hips, hands caressing her body in a way that should have been alluring, but instead disturbed.

"I just want to talk." He took a step forward, hands still raised, a wary distance between them. The figure on the bed ignored his words, her hands touching herself all over.

"Look. I'm really not interested." The desperation in his voice was a counterpoint to the forced sensuality of the room. Not wanting a barrier between him and this eerily silent woman, he reached out to pull the silk curtain aside. It tore in his hand, and strands of something sticky and coarse clung to his fingers.

"Cobwebs," he breathed, the realisation washing over

him. Not sheets of silk, but a shroud woven by the same eight-legged horrors that infested the street and the house. He'd paid for a plaything, but the true star of this twisted play waited in the shadows.

CHAPTER 25
MARIONETTES

Niamh watched, horror warring with a cold, analytical clarity. From the trapdoor in the ceiling, a monstrous spider, the size of a large dog, descended. The urge to let out a scream, just like Dani, and to engage in a fierce struggle consumed every fibre of her being. But survival meant stillness, meant being the overlooked statue in this spectacle of cruelty.

Dani was a small, huddled figure beneath the terrifying, oversized predator. She tried to move back, but the henchman held her there. The vastness of the room swallowed her cries, choked off into whimpers as a strand of silk shot out and attached itself to her back. She panicked and fought against the henchman's grip, but it remained unyielding. Then, like a marionette yanked by an unforgiving hand, the spider pulled her upward.

The sheer panic in Dani's screams as the spider drew her closer was a physical blow. It threatened to rip through the control Niamh clung to. But her only chance of escaping was to remain calm. They had to believe that she was broken.

When the spider had drawn the struggling Dani close enough, it bit her. The bite must have contained some paralysing toxin as Dani's screams abruptly stopped, and her body slumped into unnatural stillness. Then came the industrious horror of the spider, spinning its sticky shroud around Dani's face, cutting off sight and breath. When the task was completed, it dragged the limp body into the darkness above, leaving nothing but silence in its wake.

"Ye don't get used to it, do ye?" The henchman's voice was a low rumble that vibrated through Niamh's skin. She forced her eyes to maintain their empty stare.

The gentleman's response was a disdainful scowl. "Fetch the other one."

The henchman yanked Niamh from the sofa, the rough handling snapping the last fragile threads of her control. She felt the cold mask of surrender slip, a sliver of defiance replacing it.

He pushed her to her knees on the same spot as Dani had been. "Stupid cow doesn't have a clue," he sneered, his hold on her loose, almost careless. Now. There was only now.

The gentleman, his focus on the trapdoor, didn't see the predatory shift in Niamh's eyes. Neither did the henchman.

———

The webs yielded with a strange resistance that made Jack's skin crawl. He clawed at them, needing to get to the woman, to find out if some spark of humanity remained under the perverse trappings of this scene. Then, as the layers parted, something monstrous revealed itself.

The woman's face was a mask of thick, suffocating silk. Her limbs jerked and twitched with unnatural life, each movement manipulated by gossamer strands leading up into the canopy of the bed. A wave of nausea hit Jack. He'd been so focused on the horror of the brothel aspect that he'd completely missed the true masters of this place.

"Jesus fuck!" The words ripped from his throat as he

scrambled backward, eyes locked on the enormous black spider nestled in the canopy. Its eight eyes glittered with cold intelligence as it manipulated its human puppet with macabre artistry.

Panic fuelled Jack. He searched the room for an escape route, a weapon, anything. His hand brushed against his shoe and he remembered the razor. He fumbled for the concealed weapon and retrieved it. Opening it with a thumb, he extended it, a defence that was laughably inadequate, but it provided some semblance of protection.

He backed to the door.

Finding it locked, he pounded against it, his shouts echoing in the dimly lit room. "Let me out!"

The woman on the bed slumped lifelessly as the spider severed the silken strings. Freed, it turned, its bulbous body a mutated affront to nature, and scuttled toward Jack with terrifying speed.

"Help! Let me out!" His voice rose in pitch, the animal fear breaking through his calm.

The creature closed in, eight legs propelling it across the floor with a smooth, horrifying efficiency. He was trapped. A cornered rat armed with a razor meant for shaving and nothing else. He now understood the maids and bouncers and the resigned looks in the eyes of the patrons.

This was more than a brothel. It was a hunting ground. And Jack Cullinan, scared, grieving, and armed only with a straight razor, was prey.

Niamh's world shifted as another monstrous spider descended from the trapdoor. Its markings were subtly different from the other, a sign that there wasn't a single predator but an entire house of horrors. The henchman's grip tightened on her shoulder, his gaze locked on the creature above them. A low anticipatory rumble escaped his throat. Niamh could feel it in her bones - she was the next morsel on the menu.

Yet, the henchman had already discarded her in his eyes. Catatonic, broken, nothing but a body awaiting its macabre dance. His arrogance was her chance.

When the spider aimed its silent, silken weapon, Niamh surged forward, throwing off the henchman's balance, making him step into the path of the web. The henchman cried out a startled curse as thick, sticky strands wrapped around his neck.

Instinct took over. She whirled, her movement a blur, fingers finding the knife hilt at the man's belt. The weapon was free in a single motion, and she stepped out of his reach.

"You bit-" As the spider pulled the large man from his feet and lifted him upward, the henchman's words were strangled. His hands flailed to free himself. He reached for the knife at his belt, then saw it in Niamh's hand. She almost felt guilty at the betrayed look the man threw at her.

Just before the spider bit down, the man's terrified eyes pleaded with Niamh, then the gentleman. When the spider bit him, his body went as limp as Dani's had. As the spider created a silken shroud, Niamh looked at the gentleman. He froze in shock. *Shock is fleeting.*

As soon as she had the thought, the gentleman shook it off, glanced at her, and bolted for the door.

Niamh was faster. Fury drove her forward, and she caught him, the blade a cold weight against his ribs.

"No, you don't." Her voice was rough, ragged with adrenaline and the echoing screams of Dani still ringing in her ears. "You're my way out of here."

The knife was a promise, a threat. This man, this monster, held the key to her escape. The thought resonated with a fierce, dark satisfaction. The tables had turned, and she wasn't the marionette anymore. She was the one holding the strings.

The spider scuttled forward. Jack dodged a spray of gossamer silk, the sticky strands barely missing their mark. Then, with an awkward lunge, he brought the razor down, slashing blindly. The blade connected, slicing clean through a hairy leg. Greenish ichor, the spider's blood, oozed and spattered, and the creature recoiled with an unnerving hiss.

It wasn't retreating, just regrouping. Its remaining legs twitched, its body a quivering mass of vicious fury. Jack braced himself, every muscle tight. The spider lurched forward again, slowed by its injury but still terrifyingly fast. Jack backed away, waving the razor to keep the monster at bay.

He slammed at the door again, hard enough to sting the palm of his hand. A jolt of panic spiked his adrenaline even higher. Then, with a creak, the wood gave way behind him, and he tumbled backward.

He landed hard on the carpeted hallway floor. Disoriented, he scrambled upright, brushing past a startled attendant. "Hey! Watch it!"

Ignore her, his mind screamed. Slamming the door shut, he locked it and turned, gasping for breath. He was shaking uncontrollably but still gripped the razor. The thick, greenish liquid on the blade proof the fight wasn't a nightmare.

The attendant stared, a flicker of fear replacing her initial annoyance. "You'll pay dearly for that!"

Before she could raise a shout, Jack was on her, his hand clamping over her mouth, the razor inches from her eyes.

"*Shhh.* Is it worth losing an eye over?" It was all the bravado he could muster, his voice barely more than a ragged gasp.

She shook her head frantically.

"They brought a woman in earlier today. You're going to take me to her."

"But-"

He pressed the razor against her skin, drawing a pinprick of blood. "Do you know where she is?"

A whimper, a small nod.

"Good. Show me." He released her but kept the razor poised, his hand shaking despite the bravado. His time playing the role of polite customer had ended. He was a man on the edge, with madness on one side and the possibility of finding Niamh on the other.

CHAPTER 26
ESCAPE

The attendant's grip on Jack's arm tightened, her manicured nails digging into his skin as if the Devil himself were on their heels. Which, in some sense, he was.

His heartbeat pounded in his ears, reverberating through his body with every creak of the aged townhouse steps. The attendant's whinging frayed his nerves further as they descended, each footfall drawing their inevitable confrontation with the doorman, Cassius, ever nearer.

They made it to the last step before the behemoth stepped from the lounge. Jack's stomach dropped harder than any corpse he'd prepared. The hallway's dim lighting did nothing to hide the way the man cracked his knuckles like dry kindling, but it was the man's silence that terrified Jack.

"Help! He cut me!" The attendant's voice cracked. No point in playing knight in shining armour, not when he had his own skin to worry about. He shoved the woman in front of him, a makeshift shield between his body and that monster.

"No worry o' mine," Cassius rumbled, pushing the shrieking woman aside like a bothersome fly. He lunged like a bear roused from hibernation, hunger in his eyes that had nothing to do with food.

Jack's instinct kicked in. The flick of his wrist, a flash of honed steel. Somehow, he connected, leaving a gash on the back of the monstrous hand.

Cassius grunted in surprise, then made an unsettling, wet, slurping sound as he licked the wound. He grinned, a flash of bloodstained teeth. "Tastes o' spiders, it does."

Jack's face distorted in disgust. "Niamh!" he screamed, desperation clawing at his insides. The name ripped from his throat, a prayer to whatever gods might be listening.

Cassius stalked forward, each step an earthquake threatening to bring the townhouse down around them.

"Niamh! It's Jack!" he shouted as he kept the bouncer at bay, barely, with the threat of another strike from his straight razor. His only hope: the door at the end of the hall.

In a burst of noise and fury that could have split the stone, that door slammed open. And standing there, like a dark angel, was Niamh. Only, the angel had a knife pressed to the manager Tommy's throat, his eyes glinting wild and dangerous.

"Leave him the fuck alone or I cut this cunt's head off!" The words exploded from Niamh, a curse more than a command. Tommy let out a pained gasp, and Cassius paused. *Good.*

"Do as she says," Tommy wheezed, a trickle of fear leaking into his voice.

Niamh guided Tommy forward, keeping the knife steady at his throat.

Cassius shuffled backward, obeying his boss's command.

"That's right, keep going, you billy-goat-eating motherfucker!" said Niamh.

Jack darted past Niamh, taking in the sight of her in a drab grey tracksuit with that same stubborn fire in her eyes. They made a hell of a pair. But right now, he'd prefer better odds.

Cassius reached the bottom step of the stairs, a scowl replacing his bloody grin.

"Up you go," Niamh ordered, her knife hand ready to plunge into Tommy's throat.

Cassius didn't argue, backing up step by step, his gaze never leaving Niamh. At the top of those stairs, something moved into view, and Jack's heart sank even further. A nightmare of spindly legs descended. The marionette spider, all gleaming eyes and dripping fangs.

Shoving Tommy into Cassius felt damn satisfying to Niamh. The look of shock on his brutish face, the way he nearly stumbled under the witch's weight... it bought them a sliver of time. Not much, but enough. They raced to the door and opened it wide. *Thank fuck for that*, thought Niamh.

Spiders the size of dinner plates scuttled out of doorways at their heels. They swarmed around Cassius, drawn to Tommy's unnatural blood, giving her and Jack their chance.

"This way!" Jack yelled, yanking her hand and pulling her through the doorway and down onto the street. She glanced back, the sight of those scuttling monstrosities enough to make her skin crawl. Witches she could handle, but spiders? Especially unnatural ones with too many legs and glowing eyes? *Nightmare fuel.*

"Quickly now!" Jack's voice was a desperate rasp as they sprinted down Aranea Street. More spiders, smaller ones, poured out of cracks and crevices like a living, clicking wave. The cobblestones under her feet turned treacherous as the swarm thickened. There was no way around them, only through.

The crunch of spider bodies beneath her boots made her gag. If she stopped to think, to really see... well, she didn't have time for that. Jack pulled her forward, his grip reassuringly strong.

The bigger marionette spiders were gaining. "Almost there!" said Jack.

They crested the rise of the street, and relief slammed into her. Ahead, just darkness and the possibility of getting the hell out of this twisted place.

They raced hand in hand, the adrenaline pushing the horror of the spiders temporarily aside. The adjoining street was empty, thank God. A glance backward confirmed they weren't being followed, and finally, Jack's hearse came into view.

They scrambled inside, Jack fumbling at the keys while she slammed the door shut. The engine roared to life, and with a screech of tires, they sped away, leaving Aranea Street far, far behind.

———

Jack's heart pounded as Niamh's voice cut through his panic. "Easy, baby."

He whipped his head in her direction, then back to facing forward. His mouth twisted into a terrified rictus. "I thought you were fucking dead."

She rubbed his arm gently, and he felt a wave of relief wash over him. "I know, love."

He forced his face still, wiping away the tears that blurred his vision. He blinked the rest away, trying to make sense of the chaos they'd just escaped. "What happened to you? What in the name of Christ was" - he gesticulated behind them, the horrors of the brothel still fresh in his mind - "that place!"

"I have no idea. The end of the line for many." Niamh shuddered, and Jack's stomach twisted with dread. "The Sisters sent me there."

Niamh's eyes widened, and Jack's heart skipped a beat.

What else had she endured while he'd been drowning his sorrows?

"The Sisters?" he asked, almost afraid of the answer.

Niamh reached across and gripped his arm, her urgency palpable. "We have to go back."

Jack winced in pain at her grip, his battered body protesting. "What? Go back there?"

"The convent. They have our baby, Jack."

His mind reeled, trying to process her words. "What?"

"Our wedding night. I was pregnant when they took me."

"How?" The question fell from his lips before he could stop it.

Niamh looked at him incredulously. "Do I need to draw you a diagram?"

"What? No!" He paused, the weight of her revelation sinking in. "We have a baby?"

Niamh nodded, her eyes shining with love and fear. "A little girl."

"A daughter?" Jack's voice was barely a whisper, awe and terror warring within him.

"Yeah."

Fear gripped his heart, the thought of their child in the clutches of those monsters. "We have to get her."

"No shit, Jack. But I need the grimoire to do it."

"Oh." The memory of the ancient book hit him like a punch to the gut. The last piece of the puzzle he'd recklessly discarded.

Niamh stared at him intently, her gaze searching his face. "You still have it, right?"

Jack fell silent, shame and regret burning in his chest. A moment passed, each second an eternity.

"Please tell me you still have it," Niamh pleaded, her voice tinged with desperation.

———

The dim glow of the camping lantern illuminated the hearse's interior, casting shadows across Niamh and Jack as they held each other close, lying atop the sleeping bag. Niamh's eyes widened incredulously as she processed Jack's revelations.

"So, in the space of nine months, you've lost your business, abandoned your house, and lost your mind?" she asked.

Jack's crooked smile played on his lips. "At least I still have my health."

Niamh pushed him to arm's length, scrutinising his appearance. "You've looked better."

Despite her words, she pulled him close again, relishing the warmth of his embrace. They savoured the moment, their bodies intertwined, until Jack's demeanour shifted, his focus returning to the pressing matters at hand.

"Tell me about these fucking nuns," he demanded, his tone serious.

"The Sisters of Balor," Niamh replied, her voice low and ominous.

Jack nodded, encouraging her to continue.

"They'd been searching for me for a long time and had finally caught up," Niamh admitted, her forehead creasing into a frown. "But I'd found something I could use against them."

"Your family's book," Jack interjected.

"My family's spell book," Niamh corrected, her eyes narrowing. "How could you forget it?"

Jack's gaze dropped. "I didn't know."

"And then sell it?" Niamh pressed, her voice rising.

"I didn't know!" Jack repeated, his frustration clear.

Niamh sighed, resignation settling over her features. "No matter." She paused, her mind drifting to darker memories. "After they took me, they brought me back to my old room in the convent."

"Old room?" Jack asked.

"Yeah. They raised me," Niamh confirmed, her voice tinged with bitterness.

Jack's eyes widened. "Fucked-up childhood, that must have been."

"You've no idea. I ran away as soon as I could," Niamh said, shuddering at the thought. "The room was unchanged."

Jack reached out to comfort her, saying, "You're safe now."

Niamh shrugged off the gesture, her mind focused on a more pressing concern. "But she's not!" Her voice was laced with urgency.

"We'll get her back," Jack said, his resolve unwavering.

Niamh nodded, drawing strength from Jack's resolve. "Tell me about Martin Boyle," she said, changing the subject.

"He's a weasel." Jack sighed, his disdain evident. "But he doesn't ask questions." He met Niamh's gaze, his eyes earnest. "It was the last book I sold, I swear."

Niamh accepted his words with a nod. "We'll get it back."

"I can't see him giving it voluntarily," Jack said, his brow furrowed.

"We'll get it," Niamh repeated, her voice firm. She snuggled into him, her body molding to his. "Now try to sleep. We're going to need it."

As they lay together, the weight of their mission hung heavy in the air, but in each other's arms, they found a momentary respite from the darkness that awaited them.

———

Tommy examined the receipt the barman had found, his eyes narrowing as he read the store name printed at the top: Boyle's Antiquarian Books & Curios. He recognised it - that old fool, Boyle, dealt in all sorts of rare and occult objects. Tommy was curious what the man, no, the thief, had sold.

He turned to Cassius, his most trusted enforcer. "First thing tomorrow morning, I want you to pay a visit to our friend, Mr Boyle. Find out what you can about our visitor and what item this receipt is for. Bring them both back here."

Cassius nodded, his expression grim. "And if Boyle doesn't want to cooperate?"

A cruel smile played across Tommy's lips. "Then make him. I don't care what methods you use."

Cassius cracked his knuckles. "Understood, boss. I'll get it done."

Tommy dismissed him with a wave, then leaned back in his chair, steepling his fingers thoughtfully. The man had proven to be quite the troublemaker, barging into his establishment and making off with one of his new assets. But perhaps it was a blessing in disguise. Judging by the price Boyle payed for it, the object was almost certainly powerful. Tommy was sure he could find a use for it.

He would have to keep a close eye on this situation. If the thief or the woman he had taken posed any further threat, they would need to be dealt with swiftly and decisively. He allowed himself a moment to savour the anticipation, then rose from his chair, ready to set his schemes in motion. The House of Marionettes was about to enter a new era of power and influence, and he would be the one pulling all the strings.

CHAPTER 27
THE BOOK OF RAVENS

The morning sun cast a pale light over the near empty street as Martin Boyle arrived at Boyle's Antiquarian Books & Curios. His eyes darted warily at the scattered pedestrians, his body language guarded and unwelcoming. A woman walking her dog caught his attention, her gaze lingering on him a moment too long. In response, Martin hawked and spat on the ground before her, his actions deliberate and crude.

Disgust contorted the woman's face as her dog yapped at Martin, straining against its leash. She held the animal back, giving the ill-tempered shop owner a wide berth as she hurried past.

Once the woman had disappeared from view, Martin opened the shutters of his shop, the metal clanging against the storefront. He entered the dim interior, flipping the *CLOSED* sign to *OPEN* from inside, a perfunctory gesture that held little enthusiasm.

Unbeknownst to Martin, a figure had been observing the scene from a distance. Cassius stood motionless, his enormous frame draped in a trench coat. He squinted at the crumpled receipt clutched in his hand, comparing the writing on it to the shop sign before him. Satisfaction flickered in his eyes as he confirmed he had made it to the correct destination.

With purposeful strides, Cassius approached the antique shop, his massive form casting a shadow across the threshold. He crouched low, ducking his head to avoid the top of the doorframe as he entered, his presence filling the space with an air of menace.

As the door closed behind Cassius, the roar of an engine disrupted the momentary silence. Jack's hearse pulled into the parking space outside the grubby store.

———

Niamh, in the passenger side of the hearse, wore the jeans, T-shirt, boots, and leather jacket that Jack had brought from the cottage. Jack marvelled at how much more she looked her usual vibrant self.

As he readied to exit the hearse, Niamh made as though to leave, too, asking, "How do you want to do this?"

Jack sat back in the driver's seat. "I want to do this myself," he said, his voice firm but tinged with concern.

Niamh frowned. "What? Why?"

Jack took a deep breath, his gaze meeting hers. "I know Boyle. I'll have a better chance of getting it back from him myself."

Niamh raised a skeptical eyebrow, unconvinced by his reasoning.

Jack, sensing her doubt, continued, his tone growing more serious. "Besides, he's a fucking weasel... I don't want you near him or him near you."

He shook his head, struggling to find the right words to convey the depth of his feelings. Tears welled up as he spoke.

"The less you're involved in this shitshow I've created, the better."

Niamh's expression softened, her heart aching at the sight

of Jack's distress. She reached out and pulled him close, enveloping him in a comforting embrace.

"Oh, Jack," she whispered, her voice a soothing balm.

After a moment, Niamh pulled back, her eyes locking with his. Her voice was resolute as she laid out her terms.

"You've got ten minutes. If you're not out with the book by then, I'm going in."

———

The bell over the door tinkled as Jack strode into Boyle's. He marched straight to the counter and slammed down the remains of his cash. He wasn't fucking around.

"Good morning, Martin," Jack said, his voice tight. "I'm going to be needing the book back."

Martin shook his head, his expression one of profound disappointment. From under the counter, he produced a crumpled piece of paper. Jack's stomach clenched as he recognised the receipt Martin had given him only yesterday.

"For fuck's sake, Jack. What were ye thinking?" Martin demanded. He waved the gory receipt before Jack. "The House of Marionettes? That's some twisted shite right there."

A mountainous figure moved into view behind Martin. Cassius, the man-mountain from the night before, cracked his boulder-like knuckles. "Hello, little man."

Jack's hand drifted to his pocket, fingers closing around the straight razor concealed within. He eased it out, letting his thumb guide the blade open with a soft snick. Light glinted off the keen edge.

Cassius's eyes flicked to the razor before fixing back on Jack's face. "Where's your girlfriend?"

He lunged without waiting for a reply. Jack backpedalled, but Cassius's reach was too long. Meaty hands clamped around Jack's arm, reeling him in like a fish on a line. Jack slashed with the razor, but Cassius caught his wrist in an iron grip. The giant shook him violently, sending the blade flying from his hand to skitter across the floor.

Cassius smiled, cold and mirthless. Then, with no effort at all, he hurled Jack into a nearby shelf. Wood splintered and books flew as Jack crashed through it and landed on the floor, dazed.

Martin cried out in rage at the destruction.

Groaning, Jack struggled to rise, his head ringing.

———

Niamh shifted in the passenger seat of the hearse, the aged leather creaking beneath her restless form. She glanced at the clock, its hands crawling with agonizing slowness, and heaved a sigh that echoed in the confines of the vehicle. The air hung heavy with anticipation.

Her fingers drummed an impatient rhythm on her thigh, a staccato beat that mirrored the thrumming of her heart. The wait stretched on, each passing second an eternity as Niamh's mind raced with possibilities, conjuring scenarios within the bookshop that ranged from the mundane to the macabre. She shifted again, her movements jerky and uncoordinated, as if her body was rebelling against the forced inactivity.

———

Cassius hurled Jack through a bookcase, sending him crashing to the floor in a shower of splintered wood and torn pages. Jack let out an agonised groan as pain lanced through his battered body.

Under the counter, Martin cowered, his hands shaking as he fumbled with the safe's lock. Sweat beaded on his forehead, his breath coming in panicked gasps.

In one fluid motion, Cassius seized Jack by his shirt front and wrenched him off the floor. His fist connected with

Jack's jaw in a sickening crunch, catapulting him into a display cabinet. Glass shattered and books thudded to the ground as Jack slumped against the ruined shelves. Blood trickled from a gash on his forehead, staining his skin crimson.

―――――

Niamh reached over and flicked on the hearse's radio, twisting the tuner with a deft motion. Classical music drifted from the speakers, filling the vehicle's interior with its gentle strains. She wrinkled her nose. "Nope."

With another quick twist of the dial, the soothing notes switched to upbeat pop. The saccharine melody assaulted her ears, eliciting a grimace. "Yuck!"

Determined to find something tolerable, Niamh spun the knob again. This time, a twangy country tune blared forth, the singer's nasal voice warbling about lost love and pickup trucks. Rolling her eyes, she muttered, "Not today, Satan."

One more spin, and finally, the energetic pulse of rock music filled the hearse. Guitar riffs shredded the air as the driving beat reverberated in her chest. Nodding her head in time with the rhythm, a smile tugged at Niamh's lips. This would do nicely.

―――――

Cassius dragged Jack's limp body into the centre of the ruined antique shop, debris crunching under his heavy boots. Shattered glass and splintered wood littered the floor. He rolled Jack onto his back. The smaller man lay still, breath ragged.

"Now," Cassius growled. He straddled Jack, the floorboards groaning under his bulk. Leaning in close, his hot breath washed over Jack's bloodied face. "Where's the woman?"

Jack's eyelids fluttered. His cracked lips moved, a faint whisper. Cassius bent lower to listen.

Jack sprayed a mouthful of blood into the giant's face. Crimson spattered his skin and soaked into his shirt.

"FUCK YOU!" Jack spat.

Cassius's eyes narrowed to slits, jaw clenching. He spoke through gritted teeth, each word sharp as a knife, "No more nice."

Massive, calloused fists rained down in a merciless barrage, pummelling Jack's body with no hint of restraint. The sickening crack of bone accompanied each thunderous impact. Arcs of blood sprayed through the air as Jack's head whipped violently from side to side, the room spinning wildly around him in a nightmarish blur. White-hot tendrils of agony exploded through every fibre of his being with the force of each devastating blow.

Cassius's knuckles split open, smearing warm trails of viscous red across Jack's rapidly disfiguring face as the giant man's fists continued their assault. An uncontrolled, animalistic savagery burned in the depths of the towering brute's eyes, fuelling his unbridled wrath as he sought to beat the information out of his helpless, broken victim through sheer ferocity alone. Jack could only wheeze out ragged gasps and shudder helplessly beneath the onslaught, his battered body powerless against Cassius's brutal strength.

Rock music blared from the speakers as Niamh examined the knife she had taken from The House of Marionettes. She swiped the blade through the air, testing its heft and balance, acting tough. The keen tip grazed her thumb, drawing a bead of crimson blood.

"Fuck!" Niamh hissed, jamming the injured digit into her mouth to suck away the coppery taste. She checked the clock on the dashboard and shook her head, dark hair swaying. Jack was taking too long.

"Fuck it!" With a determined scowl, Niamh shoved the knife into her belt. She wrenched open the car door and sunlight spilled into the hearse's shadowy interior.

Niamh hopped out, boots thudding onto the footpath. She slammed the door closed with a resounding *THUNK* that echoed through the empty street. Squaring her shoulders, she marched forward, ready to face whatever lay ahead. The knife at her side glinted, hungry for action.

———

Niamh stepped into chaos. She froze in the bookshop's doorway, trying to make sense of the scene before her. Cassius pummelled Jack methodically in the middle of the shop. Niamh's face twisted into a snarl as she drew the knife.

She rushed behind Cassius, grabbing his coat collar in a tight grip. With her other hand, she stabbed viciously into his kidney area. Each blow made a sickening, wet sound.

Cassius roared in unexpected agony. His enormous hands flailed, trying to grab her. But Niamh moved fast, relentless. She stabbed again and again with brutal strikes, blood splattering everywhere. His movements slowed until he keeled over, lying still on the ground.

Niamh didn't let up, the only sound the wet sucking of the knife plunging in and out of flesh.

Jack's head turned weakly to look at her. "Niamh..."

She slowed, tiring, but didn't respond. Jack crawled to her on his elbows. Putting a hand on her arm, he rasped, "Baby. He's dead."

Allowing him to take the knife, Niamh let Jack slide it away before he took her in his arms.

"I could have taken him," Jack said, the effort making him cough.

Niamh smiled slightly. Then - *CLICK*. They turned to see Martin Boyle peering over the counter, a tidy sawn-off double-barrelled shotgun in hand.

"That's all very touching, but who the hell is going to pay for this mess?" Martin demanded.

Jack struggled to his feet with Niamh's help. Coughing, blood trickled from his mouth. He wiped it away with a sleeve before staggering toward the cold dual-barrels, putting himself between Niamh and the weapon.

"I'm going to need the book now, Martin," said Jack.

"You've got balls, Jack. More than I'd have given ye credit for." Martin shook his head at the dead giant on the floor. "This is an entire world of shit." His gaze returned to Jack. "What do you need it for?"

Niamh stepped around Jack. "We need it to get our baby back."

"Niamh-" Jack began.

"No, Jack. We don't have time. Every second wasted here is another she's with those fucking Sisters."

"Can you just give us the book, Martin?" Jack asked.

Martin studied Niamh as if seeing her for the first time. "Sisters? Whose sisters would that be?"

"The Sisters of Balor."

Martin's face relaxed. "Well, why the fuck didn't you say so?" He uncocked the shotgun, setting it on the countertop. Hopping down from his stool, he navigated the destroyed shop to reach them.

"Never did a greater collection of cunts walk the gods' earth than The Sisters of fuckin' Balor," Martin spat. He stopped before them, peering up at Niamh. "They have your child?"

"Our baby," Niamh said, finding Jack's hand. "Our daughter."

"Newborn?"

"Yes."

"Do you know what they want with her?"

Niamh hesitated, glancing at Jack. "They mentioned blood."

Martin grunted. Leaning in, he closed his eyes and took a long sniff of Niamh.

"Martin!" Jack warned.

Holding up a finger to silence him, Martin finished his sniff. His eyes popped open wide a moment later, and he squinted at Niamh. "That's some auld blood you have there."

Turning on his heel, Martin navigated back to the counter. He disappeared briefly, reappearing with the grimoire. He tossed it to Niamh, who plucked it deftly from the air.

"There's your spell book. May it bring you fortune," Martin said. He stood before them, short stubby legs wide, hands on hips as he looked up at the couple. "Now. What do you know of Balor?"

"Not much. One of the Fomorians?" Jack ventured.

Martin gestured for them to follow. "This way."

CHAPTER 28
BALOR OF THE FOMORIANS

Jack and Niamh stepped into a well-organised office, their footfalls muffled by the thick carpet. In the centre of the room squatted a round table, its surface bare but for a few scattered papers. A desk with a computer monitor, mouse, and keyboard stood sentinel against the back wall, flanked by laden bookshelves on either side.

Martin perched on a step, reaching for a dusty spine on one of the higher shelves. "The Fomorians were the big baddies of Irish mythology." He slammed the weighty tome down on the central table, unleashing a billowing cloud of dust.

A chorus of coughs erupted from Jack and Niamh as they waved away the swirling particles. Martin paid them no heed, flipping the book open to a page adorned with a painting of the Fomorians. The figures were malformed and horrific, their twisted bodies and leering faces the stuff of nightmares.

"Hostile and monstrous, they came from under the sea, or beneath the earth, to oppose the *Tuatha de Danann*." Martin's finger stabbed at the image of Balor, his nail tapping against the faded parchment. "And Balor - a giant with a terrible eye that wreaks destruction when opened - is their daddy."

Martin turned to the next page, a scene where Balor and company lay waste to the land. "The Tuatha de Danann fled or fucked off, giving the Fomorians free rein to wreck the place." He turned again to a painting of an epic battle, an army of women against the Fomorian forces. "But the banshees, led by The Queen of Ravens, rose against them and cast them from this world."

Jack could have sworn he'd seen a flickering glance toward Niamh when Martin mentioned 'The Queen of Ravens' but it slipped away as his brow furrowed, skepticism inscribed in the lines of his face. "But this is all mythology, right? Fairy tales?"

Martin's gaze slid to Niamh, his eyes narrowing. "Aye. Much like the Morrigan is."

Niamh's voice was steady, but her hands trembled at her sides. "What does Balor want?"

"Balor? Who the hell knows?" Martin's words were clipped, his tone sharp. He looked from one to the other, his expression grave. "But those fucking Sisters?" He paused, letting the silence stretch for a heartbeat. "Those evil witches want to bring the one-eyed bastard back and end the fuckin' world."

Silence descended, thick and heavy. Jack's voice broke through it, disbelief dripping from every word. "Oh, come on!"

Martin ignored him, jabbing a finger at Niamh. "And they'll use your blood to do it."

Tears welled in Niamh's eyes, spilling down her cheeks in glistening trails. She spun on her heel and fled the room, her footsteps echoing in the sudden stillness.

"Jesus, Martin!" Jack's voice was a growl, his hands clenching into fists at his sides.

Niamh hunkered down, leaning her back against the counter as Jack entered the main shop area of Boyle's. She stood and turned away, hiding the tears streaking her face.

"Are you okay?" Jack ventured, concern on his brow.

"That little prick," Niamh spat, venom lacing her words.

Jack moved to hold her, to offer comfort, but she shrugged him off. "What can I do, love?" he asked.

Niamh rounded on him, eyes flashing, unable to swallow her sudden rage. "Love? Fucking love? Are you serious?"

Jack gaped, mouth hanging open in shock at her outburst.

"Where was your love when I was missing, Jack?" Her voice cracked, raw pain bleeding through the accusation.

"I didn't know-" he began, but she cut him off with a sharp gesture.

"No, you didn't know" - Niamh shoved him away with both hands, putting distance between them - "but how hard did you look?"

All the fear of the past months welled up in her and she clenched her fists. She thumped him hard in the chest.

Jack winced at the impact, at the anguish fuelling her blows.

"You looked fuck all, Jack!" Another strike, harder this time as she remembered the abuse she suffered at The Sisters' hands.

Jack grunted in pain.

"Instead, you pissed your life away down the bottom of a bottle." With a final mighty thump, which carried all the pain and anguish she felt at having her baby girl taken from her, she sent him crashing to his knees.

Jack, looking like he'd gone twelve rounds against a professional boxer, knelt there waiting for her next strike.

A feeling of sorrow, and love, and loss welled up inside

her. "Oh God!" Niamh dropped beside him, regret instantly flooding her face. "I'm sorry. I'm sorry, baby."

Jack pressed a hand to her mouth, silencing her apology. "You're right. I should have looked harder for you. I should have torn the world apart looking for you."

Niamh's anger drained away, replaced by steely resolve. "Let's just get her back."

Jack nodded.

———

The bookshop lay in disarray, Cassius's sheet-covered corpse sprawled where it had fallen, blood seeping through the fabric in crimson patches. Niamh finished bandaging and treating Jack's wounds with supplies from the first aid kit. Shirtless, his battered body a canvas of cuts and contusions, Jack winced as he gingerly shrugged his shirt back on.

Martin strode in from the back office, a hold-all swinging from his hand. He dropped the bag at their feet and crouched to unzip it wide. "These might be useful. I cleaned up your knife," Martin said to Niamh. His gaze flicked to Jack. "Found that straight-razor of yours." Reaching into the depths, he withdrew his sawn-off shotgun and brandished it. "The auld crowd-pleaser might come in handy. Plenty of cartridges too." He returned the weapon and rummaged further. "The grimoire is there and some odds and ends for the road."

Rising to his feet, Martin dug in his back pocket. "Oh, and there's this." He unfurled a small paper package, revealing a mound of white powder.

Jack's brow furrowed. "What is it? Some sort of magic powder?"

A wry chuckle escaped Martin's lips. "Ha! Something like that. That there is ninety percent pure coke, lad."

"Christ, Martin." Jack shook his head in disbelief as

Martin proffered the wrap. He held up his hands, refusing to take it.

"I'm serious, Jack. A couple of sniffs of that before you head into action and you'll be rarin' to go."

They stood at an impasse, Martin's outstretched hand holding the cocaine, Jack unmoving.

Niamh's voice cut through the tension. "With the shape you're in, Jack, it can't hurt."

Surprise flickered across Jack's face at her words. With a sigh, he took the packet and stuffed it in his pocket, then hefted the hold-all. "Thanks, Martin."

"No need to thank me. Just burn that convent down around those bitches."

Jack swung the hold-all over his shoulder, its weight a reassuring presence against his back. He turned to Martin, searching for the right words. "Listen, I... I appreciate all this. Really."

Martin waved off the gratitude with a dismissive gesture. "Ah, don't mention it. Just make sure you put it to good use, yeah?" He fixed Jack with a pointed look. "And bring that little one back safe and sound."

Jack nodded, a lump forming in his throat. He extended his hand, and Martin grasped it firmly, giving it a solid shake. "We will."

Niamh stepped forward, her gaze meeting Martin's. "Thanks, Martin. For everything." She hesitated, then leaned in and pressed a quick kiss to his cheek.

Martin's eyes widened in surprise, and he cleared his throat, a hint of colour rising to his wizened face. "Right, well, you'd best be off then. Daylight's wasting and all that."

Jack and Niamh moved toward the door, the bell above it jingling as they pushed it open. Jack paused, glancing back over his shoulder. "Take care of yourself."

"Aye, you too. The both of you." Martin's gruff voice held a note of genuine concern.

With a final nod, Jack followed Niamh out into the bright sunlight. They made their way to the hearse, an unlikely chariot for their quest. As Jack tossed the hold-all into the back, he caught Niamh's eye. "Ready?"

She took a deep breath, her hand resting on the grimoire tucked under her arm. "As I'll ever be."

They climbed inside, the doors slamming shut with a sense of finality. Jack turned the key, and the engine rumbled to life. He glanced at Niamh, her face set, and felt a surge of resolve. Together, they would face whatever lay ahead and bring their daughter home.

———

The vintage hearse rumbled down the road, its engine a low growl. Jack gripped the steering wheel, his knuckles white. Beside him, Niamh munched on the food Martin had given them, her words punctuated by the crinkle of the paper bag.

"Jack?" Her voice was soft, almost lost beneath the drone of the tires on the tarmac.

"Mm-hmm?" He kept his eyes fixed ahead, scanning the road for any sign of danger.

Niamh swallowed, the sound loud in the tense silence of the car. "Promise me, if it's a choice between our daughter and me, you'll save her."

Jack's jaw clenched. Images flashed through his mind: their little girl, her cherubic face, the way her tiny hand might curl around his finger. All imaginings. And beside him, Niamh, fierce and beautiful, the love of his life. The thought of losing either of them made his heart seize.

"Would you be quiet?" he snapped, harsher than he intended. "It won't come to that."

But Niamh persisted, her gaze boring into the side of his face. "Promise me, Jack."

He exhaled heavily through his nose. "I promise."

She nodded, seeming satisfied for the moment. Jack's grip on the wheel loosened, but an additional weight settled on his chest. He glanced at his wife, taking in the determined set of her mouth, the steely glint in her eyes. At that moment, he knew he would do anything to keep his family safe.

"Same here," he said quietly. "Save her instead of me if it comes to it."

Niamh's lips curved in a sad smile. "Promise."

The word hung heavy in the air between them as the hearse sped onward, carrying them toward an uncertain fate.

CHAPTER 29
CLEAN UP

Martin wiped sweat from his brow as he surveyed the cluttered shop. Overturned furniture lay scattered across the floor, but he had cleared a path through the debris. Only one task remained: dealing with the sheet-shrouded form sprawled in the centre of the room.

He approached the body, hands on hips, considering his options. "What to do with you?" Martin grimaced at the body, his mind whirling with the implications. Whatever he did next, he had to make damn sure there wasn't a shred of evidence tying Cassius to his shop. In the seedy underbelly of Dublin's occult scene, The House of Marionettes was a name spoken in hushed whispers, second only to the infamous Sisters of Balor.

"Feckin' eejit, getting yourself killed in my shop," Martin grumbled, giving the corpse a light kick. "Now I'm the one who has to clean up your mess."

He rubbed his chin, considering his limited options. Couldn't exactly ring the Guards, not with the illicit nature of his business. And the last thing he needed was Tommy and his goons sniffing around, looking for their missing enforcer.

No, this required a more discreet approach. Something to

ensure Cassius vanished without a trace, leaving no bread-crumbs for The House of Marionettes to follow back to him.

Grasping the legs, Martin strained with all his might. Muscles bulged in his arms as his face flushed crimson, but the heavy corpse refused to yield. Gasping, he released his grip. "Jaysus."

Next, he crouched beside the body and attempted to roll it sideways. Gritting his teeth, Martin threw his weight into the effort, but once again the unyielding mass defeated him. Enraged, he lashed out with a vicious kick. "Fucker!"

Martin's gaze drifted to the rear of the shop, where a heavy metal door led to the alley behind the building. An idea took shape, a way to dispose of the body quietly and effi-ciently.

He strode to the counter and rummaged beneath it, pushing aside boxes until his fingers closed around the handle of a rusty hacksaw. It would be messy work, but it had to be done.

Hefting the saw, Martin turned back to Cassius's lifeless form, a cold practicality settling over him. The Sisters of Balor and The House of Marionettes - two powerful players in Dublin's supernatural underworld. And now, through a twist of fate, he found himself caught between them, forced to take drastic measures to protect his own skin.

As he knelt beside the body, Martin couldn't help but wonder what dark forces had drawn Jack and Niamh into this tangled web. The ancient grimoire, the missing child, it all reeked of something far more sinister than the usual occult nonsense he dealt with.

But that was a mystery for another time. Right now, he had a corpse to dispose of. The secrets of Dublin's arcane underbelly would have to wait.

Flinging aside the stained sheet, Martin knelt by the exposed ankles, a grim smile spreading across his face. He hefted the saw, testing its weight. "Now. Let's see if we can lighten the load."

The serrated teeth of the hacksaw bit into the cold, clammy flesh with a nauseating squelch as Martin began his grisly work. His hand was soon slick with a mixture of sweat and the viscous fluid seeping from the cut. He tightened his grip on the saw's handle to compensate. The rusted metal teeth tore through the flesh with a resistance that made his arm muscles scream in protest, but Martin didn't falter. He gritted his teeth, his jaw clenched so tight it ached, as he continued sawing back and forth, each stroke deeper than the last.

Sweat beaded his brow, and he slowed his pace at the bone. When the blade caught, he muttered, "Bastard!" but took it as an opportunity to catch his breath and wipe his brow with a clean spot on the covering sheet. He examined the life choices that led to this eventuality.

After a few minutes of rest, he chastised his maudlin self, "Quit moping, Martin, and get the job done." Still, he was sorry he hadn't started farther up the leg. With a burst of energy he cut through bone and then it was smooth as butter, removing the last of Cassius's ankle, then he caught his breath again. *One foot off, one to go,* he thought. He looked at the rest of the gargantuan body. "It's goin' ta be a long evening."

The convent loomed in the suburban shadows, its concrete pillars and ornate wrought iron gates standing sentinel against the night.

Jack had parked his hearse across the street. Inside, Niamh rummaged in the hold-all, retrieving the grimoire along with their weapons.

"I can't believe you were in there all this time," Jack muttered, his voice a low rasp. He accepted the shotgun and a box of cartridges from Niamh without shifting his unblinking stare.

Metal glinted as Niamh hefted her knife and Jack's straight razor, weighing the blades on her palms. "I can't believe I'm going back in," she said.

She passed the larger knife to Jack, who tucked it into his belt, then slipped the razor into her own pocket. The cool press of the weapons steadied them, a reminder of the task ahead.

Jack's fingers curled around the shotgun stock. "So. You have a plan?"

A mirthless smile twisted Niamh's lips. "Yep. We get in, take out The Sisters, rescue our daughter, and get the fuck out."

Jack nodded, a manic grin splitting his face. "Okay then. Good plan."

A sleek black car approached the convent, stopping at the gates. The gates opened, and it drove through, taillights winking as it vanished into the night.

"Come on!" Niamh hissed.

They burst from the hearse, weapons brandished, racing across the street on silent feet. Ahead, the gates gaped, a maw ready to swallow them. They slipped through as the gates closed again.

Gravel crunched under their boots as they crept along the driveway, adrenaline thrumming in their veins. The convent crouched ahead, steeped in shadow, daring them to enter.

The tinkling bell announced Tommy's entrance through the front door of Boyle's Antiquarian Books & Curios. Two marionette spiders accompanied him, branching off to either side and disappearing into the shadowy recesses of the shop.

Martin, engrossed in tidying, didn't bother to glance up. Cassius's body was nowhere to be seen.

"We're closed!" Martin called out, his voice echoing in the empty store.

Tommy ignored his declaration, his shoes clicking on the hardwood floor as he approached. "Even for an old friend, Martin?"

At the sound of Tommy's voice, Martin's eyes widened in recognition and surprise. "T-Tommy! Didn't think you ever left the lair."

A thin-lipped smile stretched across his youthful face. "Unfortunately, the help has gone missing."

He stopped before Martin, his imposing figure towering over the diminutive antiques dealer. His gaze swept the shop with obvious distaste. "Last known location? On his way to your fine establishment."

A *THUMP* resounded from one side of the shop as a marionette spider knocked something over. Martin's attention darted in that direction.

The other spider crept silently into the back office, unseen.

"You brought company?" Martin asked, his voice tinged with unease.

Tommy's smile turned nasty. "I never leave my 'lair' without them."

The rustling of plastic came from the back office, drawing their attention. Tommy fixed Martin with a piercing stare. "Have you seen Cassius?"

Martin shifted uncomfortably under his scrutiny. "Can't say as I've had the pleasure."

The marionette spider reappeared from the back office, rolling Cassius's severed head between its legs. It came to rest at Tommy's feet, the lifeless eyes staring up at the ceiling. Tommy studied the gruesome sight for a long moment before turning his unsettling smile back to Martin.

"Is that so?"

Martin stumbled backward, trying to put distance between himself and the menacing man, but the spider that had brought the head circled around, cutting off his retreat. The other spider moved to Tommy's side, its multiple eyes glinting in the dim light.

Raising his hands in a placating gesture, Martin exclaimed, "I didn't kill him! I swear!"

Tommy's expression remained impassive as he moved to the little man. "I believe you, Martin."

He took Martin's face in his hands, stooping down to look directly into his eyes. Up close, his own eyes were revealed to be multifaceted like a spider's, and his skin's unnatural greenish hue was pronounced in the shop's light. Martin observed both features keenly. "Tell me where they went, and I won't lay a finger on you."

Martin jerked his head free from Tommy's grasp, his voice trembling. "I've no clue who yer on about."

Tommy straightened to his full height, making a tut-tutting sound. "Oh, Martin. You know exactly who I'm 'on about'."

His smile sent a shiver down Martin's spine, and he stumbled back another step. With a click of Tommy's fingers, the spiders closed in on him, herding him against the wall.

"I don't know an'tin'!" Martin cried out, panic rising in his voice.

One spider scuttled up the wall, reaching the ceiling, while the other kept Martin cornered. Martin lashed out at the spider, his voice cracking. "G'wan t'fuck!"

A strand of silk shot from the ceiling spider's spinnerets, attaching to Martin's shoulders. With deft movements of its leg-hooks, the spider gathered the thread, hoisting Martin off the ground.

"No! No! NOOOO!" Martin's screams filled the shop as he struggled against the unyielding silk.

Tommy watched impassively. "Relax. There really isn't any point in struggling."

Despite Martin's frantic wriggling, the spider made quick work of securing his limbs, suspending him halfway up the wall. Tommy approached calmly, stopping a yard from his bound form. Martin was now at eye level with him, helpless and trapped.

Tommy loomed over Martin, his eyes glinting with malice. "You were about to tell me where the man and woman I'm looking for have gone."

Martin started, his voice quavering, "I don't-"

With a flick of Tommy's wrist, the monstrous spider on the ceiling skittered closer, its dripping fangs poised inches from Martin's face.

"Wait!" Martin cried out, his body rigid with terror.

Another gesture from Tommy halted the arachnid's advance. Martin slumped in his bindings, utterly defeated. "Probably doesn't matter," he muttered. "If they're not dead yet, they will be soon."

"Where, Martin?" Tommy's tone allowed no argument.

"The Sisters," Martin whispered hoarsely. "To get back their child."

A cruel smile twisted Tommy's lips. "Ah. How touching." He turned to the hideous spider perched on the wall and beckoned it forward. "Thank you, Martin."

Tommy walked to the door, the marionette spider keeping pace at his side. Behind him, the remaining spider advanced on the helpless Martin, venom glistening on its monstrous fangs.

Panic seized the small man. "Wait! You said you wouldn't touch me!"

Pausing at the threshold, Tommy looked back, his youthful face a mocking contrast to the horrors he commanded. "I won't," he purred sweetly.

Fury and despair warred in Martin's eyes. "You fuckin' cun-"

A blast of webbing from the spider smothered his futile curse.

CHAPTER 30
THE CONVENT

The convent hunkered in the darkness, its stone walls casting long shadows across the well-manicured grounds. Jack and Niamh crouched low behind a gnarled hedge, hearts pounding, breath shallow. Ten yards of open space stretched between them and the main building. No lights in the windows, no sign of movement within.

Niamh's eyes met Jack's, flashing doggedly in the moonlight. She nodded once.

They bolted from the cover of the hedge, dashing across the lawn in a frenzied sprint, their boots thudding against the earth.

At the weathered oak doors, they skidded to a halt, chests heaving. Jack grasped the wrought iron handle and turned. The hinges groaned as the door swung inward. *Thank fuck for that!* Blackness gaped before them, thick as a tomb.

Niamh glanced over her shoulder at the silent grounds, then slipped inside like a shadow. Jack followed, easing the door shut with a soft thud that echoed in the darkness.

They entered the convent's shadowy reception area, their footsteps echoing across the spacious, tiled floor. Dim light cast an eerie pall over the wooden reception counter and the wide stairways flanking it, which led up to a first-floor balcony overlooking the ground floor. Four ominous doors, all shut, led from the reception area - two on each side of the counter.

Jack's eyes darted around the gloom. "Where to?"

Niamh frowned, her gaze flicking from door to door. "I'm not sure."

"We can't stay here," he hissed.

"I know!" she said.

A thunderous clap reverberated through the reception area as the lights blazed to life, banishing the shadows. The ground floor doors flew open and four black-robed Sisters emerged, moving with unnatural speed and silence. Instead of the typical white, they wore red porcelain masks, their expressions twisted into devilish leers.

"So much for surprise," Jack muttered.

Two more crimson-masked Sisters materialised on the balcony above, leaping down with feline grace to land lithely on the ground floor. The six Sisters stepped back in unison, dropping into identical fighting stances.

"What the fuck?" Jack breathed, unease prickling his skin.

Slipping the small package from his back pocket, he opened it with his thumb and shoved it to his nose, inhaling the contents deeply. The drug hit his system like a freight train, heightening his senses and sending a surge of energy through his system.

Beside him, Niamh flipped open the weathered grimoire, swiftly finding the page she sought. "Keep them off me," she commanded, her voice low and urgent.

Jack moved to shield her, sawn-off shotgun drawn and at the ready. He glared at the assembled Sisters, a predatory gleam in his eye. "Come on, you bitches!" Jack's roar echoed through the reception area as Niamh began her incantation. Her guttural voice reverberated off the walls, an unearthly sound that sent chills down his spine. The whites of her eyes darkened to obsidian as an ethereal wind whipped her hair.

Two Sisters rushed in from the middle. Jack intercepted, firing his shotgun. The blast struck them square in the chest, hurling them backward. Cracks spiderwebbed across the ceiling high above.

Niamh's chant intensified, her voice deepening. The wind howled.

More Sisters charged in from either side. Jack fired left, scoring a headshot. The porcelain mask shattered, revealing desiccated flesh beneath. He cracked open the shotgun, ejecting spent shells. The right Sister closed in as he reloaded. She whirled into a roundhouse kick. Ducking under it, Jack snapped the gun closed and fired, blasting her leg off at the knee. She crumpled. Drawing his knife, he stabbed her through the head before re-sheathing the blade.

The ceiling fractured further, a swirling red vortex visible beyond. Gale force winds whipped the Sisters' robes. The first two regained their feet, dropping into fighting stances. Jack mirrored them, the shotgun held out like a palm strike.

Reinforcements swarmed in, but crimson energy lashed from the maelstrom above, ensnaring most of them. Agonised wails pierced the air - the first sound they'd made. One Sister evaded the tendrils, leaping at Jack. He raised his gun and fired point-blank, blasting her from the air.

Rushing to the fallen Sister, Jack held his knife over where her heart should be. "Where is our child?"

The other Sisters vanished into the vortex above. The lone survivor grabbed Jack's hand, pulling the blade into her own chest. He recoiled as a red whip seized her body and dragged it after the others. The cracks resealed, erasing all signs of battle.

Turning, he saw Niamh slump to her knees, hair settling, eyes normal once more. Jack hurried to her side. "Are you okay?"

A methodical booming arose from deep beneath them before she could reply.

"I'm fine," Niamh said, rising. "Come on."

Reloading as he went, Jack followed her through the door beside the counter, the sound growing louder with each step.

———

The convent loomed before Tommy, its stone walls and iron gates shrouded in darkness. A chill breeze whispered through the trees, carrying the faint scent of incense and decay. Tommy's arachnid companion scurried up the bars to vanish over the top in a flash of legs.

Heart pounding, Tommy approached the gate. He knew The Sisters of Balor by reputation as ones not to trifle with, but tonight he sensed that something momentous was afoot. He was loath to miss out on a chance to turn it to his advantage.

His fingers, pale and spindly in the moonlight, curled around the icy metal. With a deep breath, he climbed, scaling the barrier in swift, preternatural movements that defied human anatomy. Higher and higher he ascended, the rough iron biting into his flesh, until he reached the apex and hauled himself over.

Tommy dropped to the ground in an animalistic crouch, gravel crunching beneath his feet. Straightening, he gazed up at the convent's Gothic spires piercing the star-flecked sky. Somewhere inside those walls lay his quarry.

The spider appeared at his feet, multifaceted eyes glinting. Tommy strode forward, the arachnid skittering alongside him, an unnatural companion on this path into darkness.

———

As Jack and Niamh ventured deeper into the labyrinthine corridors beneath the convent, the booming sound resonated and intensified. The portraits of Sisters lining the walls watched them pass, their eyes casting judgment from within gilded frames. Chaotic paintings depicted scenes from ancient legends, while statues of deities and mythical Fomorian figures loomed in shadowed alcoves.

BOOM. BOOM. BOOM. The sound reverberated in Jack's chest, mirroring the nightmare that had haunted him. Niamh glanced at him, brow furrowed with concern, but he shook his head and pressed on.

The narrow corridor ended at a pair of solid oak doors. Jack reached out and gripped the handles, preparing himself. He looked at Niamh. "Are you ready for this?"

Niamh didn't hesitate. She placed her hand on top of his and nodded. They pressed down on the handles together, pushing the doors wide.

———

Tommy paused at the entrance of the convent's reception area, his eyes adjusting to the dim lighting. Suddenly, a sharp clap echoed through the room, and the space flooded with bright light. Four red-masked Sisters emerged from the ground-floor doors and two more leapt from the balcony, landing in perfect unison, their bodies poised in identical fighting stances.

Two Sisters in the centre charged at Tommy, their movements swift and precise. Yet, he paid them no heed, his attention drawn to the methodical booming sound emanating from the door to the left of the counter. As he made his way toward it, his steps were deliberate and unwavering, unaffected by the illusory fight that the Sisters persisted in, knowing that their presence was merely meant to divert his attention. The tell was their scent; they stank of magic.

Tommy's spider companion darted fearfully as one of the Sisters attacked it. But it followed Tommy's lead and scurried to catch up with him, its movements frantic and erratic.

Both of them disappeared through the door, leaving the chaos of the reception area behind.

CHAPTER 31
THE SUMMONING

The convent's gateway chamber had a layout resembling an ancient theatre, with a high ceiling and stone-hewn steps descending to a stage. An imposing altar dominated the centre of that stage. On a wall behind it, in an ornate frame carved from ancient wood, was a pool of utter blackness - the dark at the end of the universe.

Many Sisters, their porcelain masks seeming to float in a sea of black nuns' robes, rose in unison as Jack and Niamh entered through the red double doors from the hallway. Behind the altar stood The Mother, attired in a habit, but bearing an onyx mask, its surface cracked into pieces and roughly reassembled.

Jack halted inside the door, unsure of how to proceed. Niamh's frozen state was clear from a quick glance.

"We can begin," The Mother intoned. She plucked a vial of crimson liquid from the altar as The Sisters pivoted to face her.

"The Morrigan's ancient bloodline." The Mother uncorked the vial with a soft pop. "The Crone."

"The Crone," The Sisters chanted, their voices an eerie chorus.

With force, The Mother threw the blood onto the black surface behind her. It hung suspended for a breath before the darkness devoured it, sending delicate ripples across the void. She ripped away a sheet on the altar, revealing a baby squirming beneath.

"Jack!" Niamh cried, her voice strangled with horror.

The Mother hoisted the infant aloft in one hand, a wicked knife flashing in the other.

"No!" Niamh's scream ripped through the chamber.

"The Babe," The Mother declared.

"The Babe," echoed The Sisters.

The knife's point pierced the baby's flesh, drawing forth a single drop of blood and an agonised wail.

"You bitch!" Niamh snarled, breaking whatever spell she had been under.

As Niamh and Jack charged the altar, The Mother flung the child at the dark gateway.

Jack winced, expecting the crack of bones splintering, but her small body hovered in place for a moment, like a paused television program, before the void swallowed her whole.

"Nooo!" Niamh's anguished cry shattered the air.

She outpaced Jack, diving past the altar, arms outstretched toward where her baby vanished. For an instant, she hung suspended before the blackness consumed her too.

"The Mother," intoned The Mother.

"The Mother," The Sisters repeated.

Niamh disappeared into the blackness.

Jack reached the altar, rushing past The Mother.

"These aspects of the Triple Goddess unlock the gateway" - The Mother pivoted to face him - "but only love can open it."

"Only love can open it," affirmed The Sisters.

Tommy stepped from the labyrinthine halls, his marionette spider companion skittering behind. He took in the scene with a glance.

"Don't! It's what they want!" he shouted.

Jack hesitated, surprised by Tommy's sudden appearance. *What the fuck has he to do with this?* He glanced at The Sisters. They all watched him with anticipation. The atmosphere in the room was so tense that the air itself was a held breath.

"Fuck it!" Jack sucked air deep into his lungs and plunged after his wife and child.

"Fuck," Tommy muttered.

———

Swirling darkness engulfed him as he entered the void, an eternal night without end. In the chamber beyond the gateway, the scene looked frozen, distorted, and unnatural.

Jack plunged deeper, his face contorting in agony as the shadows clawed at him. Gritting his teeth, he broke through, searching for any sign of Niamh amidst the gloom. Indistinct shapes slithered and lurched in the darkness, but Niamh was nowhere to be seen.

"Niamh!" Jack's muffled cry echoed dully, swallowed by the void.

A faint voice called back, "Jack!"

A distant pinprick of light blinked on. With a whoosh of speed propelled by desperate thought, Jack hurtled toward it.

Niamh glowed like a beacon in the darkness, clutching their daughter close as monstrous creatures bore down, grasping with shadowy claws. She dodged their attacks, shielding the child.

"Jack! We're here!" Niamh's panicked shout pierced the void.

Jack materialised at their side, face twisted in fury. "No!" With one fluid motion, he drew his sawn-off shotgun and blasted the creatures, scattering them with a thunderous report.

"Go! The gateway!" He pointed to a faint glow in the

distance, their only hope of escape. Turning back, he fired again, beating back the creatures.

With a last fearful look, Niamh vanished in a flash, speeding toward the portal and the promise of salvation.

———

Niamh reached the gateway, her heart racing a million beats an hour. The distorted scene in the chamber beyond appeared unchanged from when she first entered this eternal night. She glanced over her shoulder, searching for any sign of Jack, but only darkness greeted her.

"Come on, Jack," she whispered.

She clutched her daughter to her chest, the infant's soft cries a reminder of what she had nearly lost. *Could still lose,* she reminded herself. She stared into the void, her eyes straining for any sign of movement, any indication that Jack was on his way. The seconds stretched into an eternity as she waited, her breath coming in short, ragged gasps.

The darkness pressed in on her, a tangible force that threatened to swallow her whole. Niamh's mind raced with possibilities, each more terrifying than the last. *What if the creatures had overwhelmed Jack? What if he lay broken and bleeding, lost in the endless night?*

She shook her head, trying to banish the thoughts, but they persisted, insidious whispers that gnawed at her resolve. Niamh had always prided herself on her strength, her ability to face any challenge head-on, but now, faced with this unknown, she felt a creeping sense of doubt.

The baby stirred in her arms, and Niamh looked down, her heart swelling with love and fear. This tiny, precious life depended on her, on Jack, and the thought of failing her was unbearable. Niamh knew she would do anything to protect her child, even if it meant sacrificing her own life.

But the thought of losing Jack, of facing this world alone,

was equally devastating. He had been her rock, her anchor in the storm, and the idea of continuing without him was unthinkable. Niamh felt tears prick at the corners of her eyes, but she blinked them back, refusing to give in to despair.

She stared into the void once more, her jaw set. Jack had to make it. He had to. There was no other option. Niamh drew a shaky breath, steeling herself for the unknown that awaited beyond the shimmering portal. With a final, resolute glance into the abyss behind her, she plunged back through the gateway, the ethereal light engulfing her as she crossed the threshold once more.

———

Time slowed to a crawl as Jack reloaded the shotgun, the click and snap of metal echoing through the airless black. They were alien sounds in this primal place. He cracked open the breach, ejecting the spent shells in a wisp of acrid smoke as the otherworldly creatures reformed around him, their shadowy limbs reaching for his flesh.

Jack's fingers moved with precision, sliding the fresh rounds into the chamber even as the monsters' grasping claws stretched toward his throat. Suddenly, they froze - suspended in place as if time itself had stopped. A deep, deafening hunting horn reverberated through the void, shaking Jack to his core.

As the horn's last note faded, time resumed its normal flow. The creatures withdrew from Jack, parting like a macabre sea to form a path leading directly to him, alone in the darkness. The void pulsed with anticipation, the pinpoint of light above shimmering coldly.

Just a little longer, he thought. He had to give Niamh enough time to escape the chamber on the other side of the gateway.

Gripping the shotgun, Jack peered down the path of

monsters, trying to discern what fresh horror approached. The shadows played tricks on his eyes, shapes moving just at the edge of perception.

———

Niamh collapsed to the ground outside the shimmering black gateway, twisting her body to shield the infant clutched to her chest. They were both drenched in a thick, gelatinous liquid that oozed down her skin and matted the child's wispy hair. Even here, deep within the convent's stone walls, the hunting horn's bellow reverberated in her bones.

The obsidian surface of the gateway pulsed and vibrated as if straining to contain an immense force pushing from the other side. Niamh's heart pounded in her ears as she stared at the undulating void, transfixed by dread.

The Mother raised her arms toward the vaulted ceiling in exultation. "Rejoice, Sisters!" Her voice rang out, echoing off the chamber walls. "The seal is broken!"

The Mother lowered herself to kneel before the writhing blackness, her dark robes pooling around her. "Hail, Balor, Lord of Blight!" The Mother intoned, bowing her head in reverence.

Around the chamber, the other Sisters dropped to their knees in unison, heads bowed and hands clasped. Their voices rose as one to join their leader's invocation:

"Hail, Balor, Lord of Blight!"

The chant swelled, almost drowning out the hunting horn and filling the air with electric menace. Niamh clutched her child tighter, every muscle tensed, knowing in her bones that an ancient evil was about to be unleashed upon the world. And she was powerless to stop it.

CHAPTER 32
SPAT BACK OUT

The deafening blast of the hunting horn pierced the eternal night once more. Jack's teeth vibrated. He was certain some fillings had loosened with the infernal din. With a sharp *CLICK*, he snapped the shotgun closed, the sound echoing through the endless void.

Balor's monstrous pale form emerged from the cloaking darkness, his immense size dwarfing Jack as he approached. The shadowy creatures shrank back, cowering in the presence of the Fomorian king. Balor leaned in, his massive head obscured by a tattered white shroud.

"Ah. Human," Balor rumbled, his voice ancient and terrible. "It has been aeons since my-"

Jack's arms snapped up, levelling the shotgun at Balor's face. He squeezed the trigger.

BOOM! BOOM!

The shotgun roared, twin blasts slamming into Balor's hideous visage. The giant's head rocked back as buckshot pierced the shroud and peppered his pallid flesh.

Seizing his chance, Jack launched himself toward the distant gateway, a solitary pinpoint of light in the suffocating blackness. He hurtled through the void with all the speed he could muster.

Behind him, Balor unleashed a cataclysmic roar of primordial rage. The bellow reverberated through the abyss, its force surging out in pursuit of the fleeing human. Eldritch winds buffeted Jack as he raced for the portal and escape.

———

The gateway trembled, chunks of stone and dust raining down from the ceiling as a deafening roar emanated from its depths. Niamh, undaunted, strode into the chamber, the kneeling Sisters paying her no heed as she snatched a cloth from the altar in passing. Even The Mother remained entranced, oblivious to anything but the unfolding chaos.

With deft movements, Niamh secured her wailing infant to her chest using the altar cloth. Freeing a breast, she allowed the child to suckle, her cries fading to contented gurgles. Yet the gateway's roar grew louder, breaking the momentary peace and causing Niamh to stumble back.

The gateway burst open, expelling a figure in a gush of gelatinous liquid. Jack hit the stone floor hard, sliding gracelessly into the first row of pews, his body glistening with the viscous substance.

"Jack!" Niamh cried out, rushing to his side. She hauled him to his feet, their eyes locking in a fleeting moment of shared relief.

But Jack's demeanour shifted, his gaze hardening. "Let's go!" He was already loading shells as he backed toward the exit, shielding Niamh and the child with his body. "He's coming," he warned, his voice tight with barely contained urgency. "And he's pissed." The click of the shotgun punctuated his words.

Together, they turned and fled, racing out of the ritual chamber and down the hallways as the horrific sound of an enraged old god pursued them, his fury echoing through the stones of the convent.

———

Tommy and his spider companion crept out into the inky night. The hunting horn's ominous blast froze him in his tracks. "That does not bode well," he muttered, dread coiling in his gut.

Sprinting forward, he launched himself at the gate with arachnid agility, his familiar matching his nimble climb. They dropped to the other side and dashed across the deserted street, melting into the shadows of a narrow alley.

Heart pounding, Tommy pressed his back against the rough brick, peering at the convent's entrance through the gloom. The horn's menacing echo still hung in the air, an unspoken threat carried on the wind. His mind raced, trying to decipher its meaning as his eyes strained to penetrate the shadows.

Tommy's instincts urged him to return to The House of Marionettes to ensure the safety of Madam Arnott and their spawn from whatever unholy force had been unleashed. Yet, he fought against the urge, knowing that ignorance could be their downfall. *Forewarned is forearmed,* he thought.

He scanned the convent entrance for any signs of danger. The hunting horn's echo still reverberated in his bones, a reminder of the ancient powers at play.

The spider crouched motionless at his feet, its glassy eyes glinting with unnatural intelligence. Tommy knew they were in grave danger, but the nature of the peril remained elusive. All he could do was watch and wait with bated breath. Every muscle tensed to flee or fight as threats revealed themselves.

———

Darkness shrouded the gateway, the inky void broken only by the faint, wavering glow emanating from the portal's edges. A twisted abomination clambered forth from the shimmering surface, its form an unsettling amalgam of shadow and glistening, raw flesh. The creature flopped gracelessly onto the stone floor with a sickening thud.

Another followed close behind, and then another, until a writhing mass of horrors filled that end of the chamber. The Sisters huddled together, uncertainty and dread revealed by the uncharacteristic behaviour.

The Mother stepped away from the altar, her movements fluid and purposeful. She approached the writhing mass of creatures, her arms outstretched in a gesture of inclusion. "Welcome, brothers and sisters," she began, then reconsidered her choice of words. "Welcome, brethren... to the mortal realm."

The creatures before her were primal, their forms unsettling. They did not show any understanding of her words, their movements erratic and uncoordinated as they flopped and slithered across the stone floor.

Amidst the uncertainty and dread that hung heavy in the air, one Sister rose to her feet, her enthusiasm the opposite of the trepidation shown by the others. "Hail, Balor!" she cried out, her voice ringing clear and strong, echoing off the cold stone walls.

The Mother's eyes gleamed with approval at the Sister's bold proclamation. She seized upon the moment, her own voice rising to join the chant. "Hail, Balor!" she intoned, her words reverberating through the chamber, mingling with the unearthly sounds of the creatures before her.

The other Sisters, emboldened by The Mother's lead, joined in the chant, their voices rising in a discordant chorus of praise and reverence. "Hail, Balor! Hail, Balor!" they cried out, a declaration of their loyalty to the ancient evil they served.

The Mother stood tall and proud amidst the chaos, her eyes fixed upon the writhing mass of creatures before her. She knew that this moment marked a turning point, a new chapter in the history of The Sisterhood.

———

Beyond the veil of reality, within the eternal night of the void, Balor loomed. His massive form dwarfed the tiny gateway, an insignificant peephole in the fabric of existence. Peering through the portal, he observed his minions' exodus onto the chamber floor and the subsequent hail to him from those who waited on the other side.

Balor considered The Sisters, those devoted acolytes who had toiled for centuries to bring about his release. A cruel smile played across his hideous visage as he contemplated their unwavering loyalty. For countless ages, they had laboured tirelessly, performing the arcane rituals and sacrifices necessary to weaken the barriers that held him captive. Their dedication was admirable, and yet, Balor could not help but feel a twinge of disdain for their frailty.

He mused upon their service, wondering what reward would fit such devotion. Perhaps he would grant them a measure of his power, elevating them above the pitiful creatures they once were. Or maybe he would consume them, their essence fuelling his own dark desires.

Balor's mind turned to the world beyond the gateway, a realm he had not trod upon since the ancient days when The Morrigan had banished him to this accursed void. He yearned to feel the earth beneath his feet once more, to taste the sweet air of the mortal plane, and to sow chaos and destruction across the land.

Yes, he thought, *The Sisters had done well in facilitating his return.* Their loyalty would be rewarded, one way or another. He had a world to conquer, a score to settle with those who had imprisoned him for so long. Balor's anticipation grew as he prepared to exit the gateway, ready to unleash his malevolent might upon the unsuspecting mortals.

His frustration mounted as he realised the gateway's inadequacy. The small size couldn't accommodate his immense frame. With a growl of determination, he reached his gnarled hands into the portal, gripping its edges with crushing force. Straining against the unyielding boundaries of reality, Balor sought to force his way through, his dark will pitted against the very laws of nature.

CHAPTER 33
THE AULD GOD RISES

Jack hurried through the twisted hallways beneath the convent. The ancient stone walls closed in around him. Niamh followed close behind, her footsteps echoing off the floor. In her arms, the baby suckled, oblivious to the dangers lurking in the shadows.

A deep rumbling shook the earth, sending tremors through the labyrinthine passage. Dust rained down from the ceiling, coating their hair and clothes in a fine layer of grit. Jack and Niamh exchanged worried glances, their eyes wide with fear. Without a word, they quickened their pace, desperate to escape the subterranean maze before it collapsed around them.

The air was thick, making each breath a struggle. The darkness pressed in from all sides, broken only by the feeble light of the occasional bare light bulb, which flickered as the passage shook, casting grasping shadows on the walls.

As they ran, the rumbling intensified, the walls shaking with increasing violence. Cracks appeared in the masonry, widening with each passing second. The ground beneath their feet shifted and buckled, threatening to give way at any moment. They stumbled and staggered, fighting to keep their balance as the building crumbled around them.

———

Balor's pale hands gripped the edges of the ancient gateway, his unnatural strength splintering the ancient wooden frame and grinding the rock wall it hung upon to dust. Chunks of stone and timber plummeted through the widening portal into the endless abyss of the void.

He watched The Mother and her Sisters move back as the chamber shook. His advanced guard still floundered on the ground, not yet able to stand with their newfound weight.

Gnarled fingers traversed the gateway's edge and one hand dug into the base while the other clawed at the gateway's apex. With all the force of a god, Balor pushed the edges apart. The convent's foundations groaned in protest as the ceiling fractured within the chamber and collapsed, raining debris.

The Mother spoke and, albeit muffled, from his side of the portal he could just make out her words.

"Leave!" she commanded, her voice cracking like a whip.

"But-" a Sister protested, frozen in fear.

"Now!"

At The Mother's sharp order, The Sisters' paralysis broke. They turned and glided out of the crumbling chamber, habits billowing as they fled the unfolding catastrophe. Balor didn't worry about their abandonment; he would give them their reward once he was free.

The gateway yawned ever wider under Balor's relentless assault, an obsidian mouth swallowing the world. Eldritch darkness leaked through the breach, tainting the consecrated ground. Timeworn wards flared and sputtered out, their protection spent, as he destroyed the frame's confinement.

The convent shuddered, its ancient stones groaning as the forces of a birthing god wrenched at its foundations. From high above, the central building appeared to collapse inward, as if a giant hand had reached down and crushed it like a flimsy cardboard box.

A swirling vortex yawned open beneath the night sky, a gaping maw of darkness that swallowed everything. Through this unholy gateway, a monstrous figure emerged. First an arm, pale and muscular, clawed its way into the mortal realm. Then a shoulder, broad and powerful, heaved itself through the rift.

Finally, a head appeared, shrouded in a tattered white sheet that fluttered in the unnatural wind. Balor had arrived, an ancient evil summoned forth from the depths of the void.

He stood in the crater in the centre of the ruined convent, his white-shrouded face turning slowly as he surveyed his new domain. His limbs were sluggish, but he would grow accustomed to them again.

The hunting horn sounded from within the void. Its notes echoed across the sleeping city, announcing the return of the old god. The air trembled at Balor's presence, as if the fabric of reality itself recoiled from his touch.

As the demon lord climbed into the world of the living, his army of minions spilled from the gateway, flopping to the ground at its edge. Alongside them, a human figure stepped through.

CHAPTER 34
THE HEARTSTAFF WIELDER

The convent trembled as if gripped by a massive earthquake as Jack and Niamh sprinted from the labyrinth into the reception area. The floor pitched and heaved beneath their feet. Niamh stumbled, but Jack's hand shot out to steady her. Their eyes met for a fleeting instant, a wordless moment of gratitude passing between them before they bolted for the doors and burst out into the night.

Seen from above, the two desperate figures fleeing the convent might have been mistaken for scurrying ants. The main building, an inky silhouette against the starry sky, rose behind them. At the gateway, Balor climbed the rubble, finally free from centuries of slumber. The monstrous form was almost free of the crater and tore the remaining buildings down as he clawed his way into the world.

Jack and Niamh reached the convent's front gate, iron bars offering a pitiful illusion of safety. Behind them, The Mother and The Sisters fled the main convent building as it crashed down in their wake.

Jack pulled on the gates, but they wouldn't budge. "Fuck!"

His eyes fell on a side door to the left of the main gate and the padlock dangling from the bolt. "This way!"

———

Lorcan Crowley stood among Balor's twisted minions at the edge of the enlarged gateway. Wind caused his long grey hair and full beard to dance and he closed his eyes to the sensation. How long had it been since he felt a breeze on his face? He inhaled a lungful of air, then exhaled. *So long since I've breathed fresh air!*

Grasping the twisted staff, its blackened Heartstone crowning the top, he used it to support his weight as he re-acclimated to the burden of a corporeal form once more.

More creatures pushed through the gateway and forced him further into the world. He went gladly. He was happy to have the void at his back. Three steps in was enough for him to decide the terrain was impossible to navigate. He had neither the strength nor the size of his Lord Balor to climb out of the pit. But he had learned a trick or two in his time within the void.

Lorcan gripped the twisted staff, feeling its power pulse through his veins. He closed his eyes and reached out with his mind, tapping into the dark magic that had sustained him for so long in the void. The staff responded, its energy swirling around him like a malignant tempest.

A simple mental exertion from Lorcan commanded the shattered remnants of the crumbling convent to levitate, whipping into a frenzied cyclone of pulverised stone and billowing dust. The raging maelstrom ensnared the twisted, misshapen monstrosities clawing their way through the newly opened gateway, their grotesque forms adding to the swirling pandemonium. As he wielded this immense force with but a thought, a sinister smile played across Lorcan's lips, savouring the intoxicating rush of unbridled power coursing through his fingertips.

He focused his will on the swirling cloud, shaping it into a platform beneath his feet. The dust and debris coalesced, forming a solid surface that lifted him from the depths of the pit. Lorcan rose steadily, the staff glowing with an eerie light as it channelled the dark magic.

Ascending higher, Lorcan's gaze swept over the surrounding devastation. What was once the convent's imposing structure now lay shattered in heaps of rubble, its mighty walls brought low. The pulsating gateway to the void throbbed with violent energy, continuing to disgorge more of Balor's vile servants into the mortal plane.

Lorcan's feet touched the ground at the edge of the pit, and he stepped off the swirling cloud of debris. He planted the staff firmly on the earth, feeling its power thrumming through the ground.

He had a mission to fulfil, a destiny to embrace. With Balor's power at his command and a legion of void creatures at his side, he would bring darkness and despair to the mortal world. The age of the Fomorians had begun, and Lorcan Crowley would be its herald.

———

BOOM! The side door of the convent exploded open, shattering the night's stillness. Jack burst through to the street, Niamh close on his heels, their ragged breaths tearing at the air. They raced for the waiting hearse, its black metal gleaming under the moonlight.

Wrenching open the doors, Jack and Niamh flung themselves inside the musty interior. Jack's hands trembled as he jammed the key into the ignition, the engine roaring to thunderous life like a furious beast awakened from slumber.

Jack looked at Niamh, panic in his eyes. "Where will we go?"

"I don't know. Just drive."

He slammed his foot down on the accelerator and the tires screeched in protest against the tarmac, propelling the vehicle forward. Jack gripped the steering wheel with white knuckles, praying fervently that they would make it to safety unscathed.

CHAPTER 35
THE MOTHER'S REWARD

On top of the rubble, Balor rose to his full thirty-foot height, a towering monstrosity silhouetted against the night sky. Behind him, in the pit, a surging wave of creatures continued to pour forth from the gateway, so many they obscured the rubbled ground.

In that moment, the hunting horn bellowed again, reverberating through the darkness and announcing his coming. The synchronicity filled him with joy.

Balor strode down from the mountain of rubble that had once been a holy sanctuary, his titanic form casting a long shadow. Awaiting him on the lawn were The Mother and her Sisters spread out behind her in ranks. As he reached the level ground, they kneeled before him and chorused, "Hail Balor, Destroyer of Worlds!"

Balor surveyed The Mother and her Sisters, his single eye narrowing as it swept over their assemblage. These women, these devotees, had laboured for centuries to free him from his prison, and now they prostrated themselves before him, hailing him as their lord and master.

"Rise," Balor commanded, his voice a deep rumble that

shook the earth. The Mother and her Sisters obeyed, standing tall and proud in the face of their towering god.

"You have done well," Balor continued, his tone almost grudging. "Your tireless efforts have finally borne fruit, and I am free once more to walk this mortal realm."

He paused, letting his words hang in the air. The Mother and her Sisters remained silent, waiting with bated breath for their master's next proclamation.

"Such loyal service would typically warrant a reward," Balor mused, his massive head tilting to one side as he considered the gathering below him. "And yet..."

The Mother and her Sisters exchanged nervous glances, unsure of what their lord was implying.

"And yet, I recall it was your Order, in ages past, that aided The Morrigan in casting me and my brethren into the void."

A collective gasp rippled through the ranks of The Sisters, and even The Mother was taken aback by this revelation.

"You may not remember it," Balor continued, his voice growing colder with each word. "The passage of time has a way of erasing such inconvenient truths. But I remember. I remember the role you played in my imprisonment, and I do not forget such betrayals."

———

The Mother staggered back as Balor's words released a torrent of fragmented memories. Disjointed images assaulted her mind - a procession of ethereal figures cloaked in mist, their keening cries echoing through ancient stone passages. The Mother saw herself among them, fulfilling their sacred duty of guiding the newly deceased through a veil of shimmering light to the afterlife. *We... we were banshees?*

She cried aloud, "No!" But there was no denying the truth of it. She remembered.

Flashes of sacred rituals flickered before her eyes - chanting in a long-forgotten tongue, the scent of burning herbs, and the weight of a staff in her hand. The visions shifted, revealing megalithic structures rising from the earth, their purpose suddenly clear to her.

As the memories continued to flood in, a profound sense of loss overwhelmed The Mother. The realisation that she and her Sisters once held a sacred duty, now tainted by the atrocities they had committed in Balor's name, filled her with anguish. The weight of centuries of misguided devotion crashed down upon her, and she fell to her knees, her mask slipping to reveal a desiccated face full of grief.

The Mother's mind reeled as she grappled with the enormity of her past actions. With each passing moment, the visions grew more vivid - a battle of cosmic proportions, where a great queen, The Morrigan, led the charge against Balor and his army. She saw herself and her sister banshees standing alongside their queen, their combined power banishing the dark entities to the void. In that moment, she understood the true cost of their victory: the sacrifice of their queen and losing their identity and purpose in exchange for casting the monstrous Balor away.

The Mother crumpled to the ground and wept.

———

Balor regarded the crumpled form of The Mother with amusement and contempt. Her pitiful weeping only highlighted the depths of her ignorance and the folly of her devotion. He savoured the moment, relishing the power he held over these pathetic creatures who had once dared to stand against him.

A wicked idea formed in Balor's mind, a fitting punishment for The Sisters' former betrayal. He would grant them their old task, the sacred duty they had so carelessly abandoned in their misguided war against him. They would once again gather the dead and guide them to the ancient sites, but with a new purpose.

Balor's voice boomed across the ruins of the convent, his words dripping with malice. "You will resume your old task, Sisters. The dead shall walk the earth, and you will become abominations, forced to inhabit their bodies as shadows instructing them to do your bidding."

The Mother looked up at Balor, her eyes wide with horror as the implications of his decree sank in. The Sisters, too, recoiled at their new fate, their bodies trembling with fear and revulsion.

Balor's laughter echoed through the night, a sound that froze blood and made even his own minions cower in fear. He revelled in The Sisters' anguish, knowing that their suffering had only just begun.

Balor's single eye blazed with vengeful power as he focused his gaze upon The Mother and her Sisters. The ancient Fomorian king had waited millennia for this moment, and now, with his freedom secured, he would mete out a fitting punishment for their betrayal.

The Mother and The Sisters cowered before Balor, The Sisters' faces concealed by their masks but the Mother's etched with despair. They had devoted centuries to his cause, believing that their actions would bring about a new age of darkness. But now, faced with the true nature of their master, they realised the depths of their folly.

From Balor's terrible eye surged a wave of inky darkness, engulfing The Mother and her Sisters. Their screams echoed through the ruins of the convent as the shadows consumed them, twisting and warping their bodies into twisted, new forms.

For a fleeting instant, The Sisters revealed their true nature. Their faces, once hidden behind porcelain masks, contorted into the visages of wailing banshees. Their hair billowed around them like wispy tendrils of mist, and their mouths opened wide in silent screams.

But the moment was short-lived. As quickly as the banshees had appeared, they dissolved into tendrils of black smoke. The shadows swirled and danced as if alive with malefic purpose before sinking into the ground, leaving no trace of The Sisters' presence.

In their wake, a pile of discarded nuns' habits and abandoned porcelain masks lay strewn across the lawn. The once pristine robes had become tattered and stained, revealing the corruption that had festered within the convent for centuries.

Balor surveyed the scene with satisfaction, his eye glinting with cruel amusement. The Sisters had served their purpose, and now they would continue to do his bidding, even in death. The shadows that had consumed them would spread across the land, gathering the dead wherever they went.

"But you will need the dead to gather," he said.

Balor strode across the lawn, his immense form casting a shadow that devoured the moonlight. His eye, now uncovered, blazed with a cruel power that made the air crackle with energy. The ancient Fomorian king had waited centuries for this moment, and now, with his freedom secured, he would unleash his terrible might upon the world.

As he approached the convent's front gate, Balor saw a crowd of curious onlookers gathered, drawn by the destruction of the buildings. They gawked at the ruins, their sleepy faces fearful and fascinated. Balor's lips curled into a sneer, disgusted by their weakness and ignorance.

With a casual gesture, Balor pushed against the gateway, his strength shattering the iron bars, sending chunks of stone flying. Balor's blow crumbled the wall to either side, and those unfortunate enough to be standing too close were crushed beneath the falling debris. Screams of terror and agony filled the night air as the crowd stumbled back, fleeing from the wrath of the monstrous being before them.

But escaping from Balor's gaze was impossible. He fixed his terrible eye upon the crowd, and wherever his baleful stare fell, people withered and collapsed, their life force draining away in an instant. Within moments, scores of corpses littered the surrounding ground, their bodies contorted in the throes of death.

Balor knelt down, his massive form dwarfing the fallen. He plunged his fingers through the pavement and into the earth. A wave of blight spread out from his touch, a growing circle of decay and rot. Grass withered and died, and the soil turned black and lifeless. But as the blight reached the corpses, tendrils of darkness snaked up from the ground, writhing and coiling like serpents. They entered the bodies of the dead, infusing them with a sliver of dark energy.

Slowly, the corpses twitched to life, their limbs jerking like macabre marionettes. One by one, they rose to their feet, their eyes glazed and empty, their faces slack and lifeless. They stood before Balor, a silent army of the dead, ready to do his bidding.

CHAPTER 36
HUNTING THE PREY

Lorcan knelt before Balor, his twisted staff clutched in his gnarled hands. The ancient Fomorian king towered over him, his single eye blazing with malevolent power, but it had limited means of compelling him.

Balor's voice boomed through the ruins of the convent. "Find the child, Heartstone wielder."

For a moment, Lorcan was adrift in time, his mind reeling with fragmented memories. Had Balor ordered him to pursue his long-dead wife, Nemhain, and their son, Cormac? The images blurred, and Nemhain's face merged with that of Fea Murrigan, the woman he had saved by entering the void all those years ago in 1888. Fea bore an uncanny resemblance to his beloved Nemhain.

Lorcan shook his head, the fog of centuries lifting. *Fea would be long dead now, as dead as Nemhain and Cormac.* Grief threatened to overwhelm him, the weight of the years he had lost pressing down upon him, a suffocating burden of sorrow and regret.

"Do not try me, Wielder!"

Balor's growl snapped Lorcan back to the present. He bowed his head, his grey hair falling like a curtain around his weathered face. "Yes, my lord," he rasped, his voice rough from disuse. "I will find the child."

Lorcan rose to his feet, leaning on his staff. He turned away from Balor, his eyes scanning the devastation that surrounded them. The convent lay in ruins, the once imposing stone walls reduced to rubble. The twisted creatures, more used to their physicality, clambered through the debris, their bizarre forms shining in the moonlight.

Lorcan closed his eyes, reaching out with the staff's power. *My power!* Like a siren's song, he felt the lingering traces of the child's presence, a faint thread that called to him. He opened his eyes, a grim smile twisting his lips. He knew where to begin his search.

———

Tommy stood in the shadows of the alley, paralysed as he watched the monstrous Balor unleash destruction upon the crowd. The screams of the dying filled the air as their flesh withered and they dropped one by one to the ground. Tommy's eyes widened in horror as he witnessed the bodies of the fallen rise, their lifeless eyes staring blankly as they joined Balor's silent army.

But the man kneeling before Balor filled Tommy with a chilling dread. He squinted, trying to make out the man's features in the dim light. As recognition dawned, Tommy's breath caught. *It can't be.* The man who had murdered his beloved sister, Margarett. The man he had prayed into life on countless nights so he could exact his vengeance was alive and in league with this abomination.

"Lorcan Crowley," said Tommy.

The name tasted like ashes on his tongue. Images of Margarett's body, drained of life, flashed through his mind, the memory of her lifeless eyes staring up at him as he cradled her in his arms. The pain of that loss had never faded, even after all these years.

Tommy's hands clenched into fists, his nails digging into his palms. The urge to rush forward and tear Lorcan limb from limb was hard to resist. He wanted to feel the man's bones snap beneath his fingers, to watch the life drain from his eyes as he exacted his long-awaited revenge.

But Tommy forced himself to remain still, his body trembling with barely contained rage. He knew he couldn't face Lorcan alone, not with Balor and his army of the dead nearby. He needed to bide his time, to wait for the right moment to strike.

As Lorcan rose to his feet and strode away, Tommy's eyes followed him, burning with hatred. He would have his vengeance, no matter the cost. He forgot about Madam Arnott and the brothel, his mind consumed by the need to make Lorcan pay for what he had done.

Tommy melted back into the shadows, his spider companion skittering at his heels. He would follow Lorcan, watch his every move, and when the time was right, he would strike. The man who had taken everything from him would finally face justice, and Tommy would be the one to deliver it.

———

Jack pushed the vintage hearse to its limits, the engine roaring as they sped through the night. Beside him, Niamh cradled the sleeping child. Exhaustion carved lines on their faces, but a sense of contentment radiated from them both. Niamh tore her gaze from the baby to regard Jack, her expression serious.

"What will we name her?" Niamh asked.

Jack pondered for a moment, his brow furrowed in thought. "How about Kali?"

"Kali?" Niamh repeated, a hint of curiosity in her voice.

A slight smile tugged at the corners of Jack's mouth as he glanced in the rearview mirror. "The goddess of destruction."

Niamh's lips curved into a matching smile. "That might work."

Out of nowhere, a powerful female voice echoed in their minds, speaking to them, "*I have a name, daughter.*"

They exchanged astonished looks, eyes wide with disbelief.

"Did you hear that?" Niamh gasped.

"What the hell?" Jack muttered, his knuckles whitening as he gripped the steering wheel tighter.

In unison, they stared at the baby, no longer asleep. Her eyes shone with an otherworldly golden light, piercing through the darkness of the hearse.

"*I am Morrigan,*" the voice declared. "*I will heal this world.*"

Amazement and nervousness danced across Jack's and Niamh's faces as they shared a glance, the weight of the revelation settling upon them.

Morrigan gurgled, the sound incongruous with the gravity of her proclamation. Her eyes had returned to their regular, non-glowing hue.

"Well..." Jack said, in awed acceptance. "That's settled then."

Niamh held Morrigan close to her chest, the baby's warmth seeping through her shirt as Jack sped up, the hearse surging forward with renewed purpose.

Through the rear window, the city behind him plunged into an abyss of darkness, the once vibrant metropolis succumbing to the encroaching shadows.

CHAPTER 37

SHADOW APOCALYPSE

Balor watched with satisfaction as his minions, now accustomed to the mortal realm, poured forth from the edges of the gateway pit. They moved with purpose, their twisted forms adapting to the unfamiliar terrain as they spread out into the city, an unstoppable tide of darkness and chaos.

The creatures scuttled and slithered through the streets, their unearthly shrieks piercing the night air. Balor could sense the panic and terror that followed in their wake, the mortals' screams music to his ancient ears. He revelled in the destruction, the first taste of the power he would wield in this world.

As his minions ventured further into the city, Balor caught glimpses of their handiwork through their eyes. Cars overturned and burst into flames, their occupants dragged out and consumed by the ravenous horde. Buildings crumbled under the onslaught, glass shattering and concrete cracking as the creatures tore through them with ease.

The undead spread into the city, too, turning the unwary and driving the rest before them. And any new corpse became infused with a sliver of his corrupt power and rose to do his work as well.

He laughed. "The Shadow Sisters will be busy."

Balor's lips curled into a cruel smile as he watched the mayhem unfold. This was only the beginning, a small taste of the devastation he would unleash upon this world. With each passing moment, his strength grew, fed by the fear and suffering of the mortals below.

The gateway pit continued to spew forth more of his twisted creations, an endless stream of nightmarish beings eager to do his bidding. They swarmed the streets, their numbers growing with each passing second, an unstoppable force that would soon consume the entire city.

Balor knew that this was just the first step in his grand plan, a mere prelude to the horrors he would unleash. With his minions at his command and the power of the gateway at his fingertips, he would bring this realm to its knees, and all would tremble before the might of Balor, the Lord of Blight.

The screams of the mortals and the chaos that engulfed the streets were like a symphony to his ears, a testament to his power and the fear he instilled in the hearts of men. As he stood at the centre of the spreading corruption, a group of freshly spawned creatures gathered around him, their bodies writhing with eagerness to serve their master. Balor's lips curled into a cruel smile as he regarded them, knowing that he could put them to good use in his quest to bring darkness and despair to this world.

With a wave of his hand, Balor summoned a swirling cloud of dirt and dust and rubble, the particles dancing and twisting in the air before him. The minions watched in awe as their master's power manifested, their eyes glinting with a hunger for destruction.

Balor reached out with his mind, his corrupting energy seeping into the earth beneath his feet. He could feel the land itself recoil from his touch, the soil and rock crying out in agony as his evil power seeped into their very essence.

With a gesture, Balor pulled the minions into the swirling cloud, their forms merging with the dust and dirt until they were no longer distinguishable as individual beings. The cloud pulsed and throbbed with an unnatural energy, a living, breathing entity infused with Balor's power.

"Comb the lands and all you touch will die," Balor commanded. "Turn the living into the walking dead."

The cloud rolled away, growing larger as it moved through the streets of Dublin. A hunting horn sounded out from within it. It consumed everything in its path, leaving a trail of decay and death in its wake. The living fell before it, their flesh withering and their eyes turning milky white as they transformed into shambling corpses.

A rumbling laugh escaped Balor's lips as he watched the cloud disappear into the night, knowing that it would bring more dead for the Shadow Sisters to gather. He envisioned the city as his own personal playground, where he could indulge in his sinister desires, and anyone who dared to challenge him would face swift and merciless defeat.

———

Madam Arnott's eyes snapped open, her senses attuned to the chaos engulfing the city beyond the walls of The House of Marionettes. She lay still, her body entwined with the arachnid reproduction system that had been her constant companion for a century. The air crackled with an unseen energy, and Madam Arnott knew something momentous had occurred.

She waited, expecting Tommy to come to her as he always did, ready to attend to her needs. Minutes ticked by, stretching into an hour, and still, Tommy did not appear. A flicker of unease stirred within Madam Arnott as a troubling thought took root in her mind. *Perhaps Tommy would never come.*

With a surge of strength that had lain dormant for decades, Madam Arnott began the agonising process of detaching herself from the reproduction system. Each movement sent waves of pain through her body, but she gritted her teeth and persevered. Slowly, inch by excruciating inch, she pulled herself free from the arachnid embrace.

At last, Madam Arnott tumbled to the ground, her naked body coated in a layer of thick, viscous mucus. She lay there, gasping for breath, as the cold air hit her exposed skin. The unnatural bond she had endured left angry red welts on her pale skin where her flesh had fused with the reproductive system.

Despite the pain and the rawness of her wounds, Madam Arnott realised she was otherwise unharmed. She pushed herself up on shaking arms, her muscles weak from years of disuse. As she sat there, naked and vulnerable, Madam Arnott felt a flicker of her old strength returning, an ember of the formidable woman she had once been.

She struggled to her feet, her legs trembling beneath her as she tried to stand. The years spent confined to the reproduction system had taken their toll, leaving her muscles atrophied and weak. She swayed, her balance precarious, and felt herself falling back toward the floor.

Without warning, a swarm of marionette spiders entered the room, their spindly legs carrying them swiftly to Madam Arnott's side. They surrounded her, their bodies forming a living scaffold that supported her weight. With their help, Madam Arnott found the strength to move forward, each step a little more confident than the last.

Together, she and the marionette spiders left the dark, hidden room that had been her self-imposed prison for so long. They navigated the twisting corridors of The House of Marionettes, the spiders guiding her to her old room. As they moved, Madam Arnott felt a sense of familiarity wash over her, memories of her past life stirring in the depths of her mind.

When they reached her room, she pushed open the door with a trembling hand. It was just as she remembered it, a reminder of the life she had once led. She approached the wardrobe, the marionette spiders parting to allow her passage. With each item of clothing she donned, Madam Arnott felt her strength returning, her body remembering the motions of dressing herself.

Once clothed, she turned to face the marionette spiders. They chittered, their eyes gleaming in the dim light. She knew they could sense the chaos unfolding in the city, the same turmoil that had stirred her from her long slumber. With a nod of gratitude, she left her room. The spiders trailing behind her.

As she stepped out of The House of Marionettes, the frosty air caressed her skin. She breathed, relishing the sensation of freedom. In the distance, the city was in upheaval. The sounds of sirens and screams carried on the wind. Madam Arnott knew she had to leave, to put as much distance between herself and the approaching chaos as possible.

With the marionette spiders at her side, she walked, her steps growing more confident with each passing moment. She headed away from the city toward an uncertain future, but one that was hers to shape.

CHAPTER 38
EOIN AND BRENDAN

Eoin sat slumped on the couch in the living room of the apartment he shared with his girlfriend, Dierdre. Technically, it was Dierdre's apartment, but Eoin didn't bother too much about that detail. Eoin's fingers skillfully manipulated the controller as he guided his character through a zombie-infested town in his latest first-person shooter game, his eyes fixed on the television screen. Gunfire and explosions filled the room, punctuated by the occasional curse from Eoin when his character took a hit.

He shifted on the couch, his nose wrinkling as he caught a whiff of his own body odour. He'd been wearing the same clothes for days, too engrossed in the game to bother with trivial things like hygiene. Eoin reached for the large joint resting in an ashtray on the coffee table, bringing it to his lips and taking a deep drag. The smoke filled his lungs, and he held it there for a moment before exhaling slowly, watching the tendrils of smoke curl and dissipate in the air.

A loud bang from outside the apartment caused Eoin to jump, his heart racing. He paused the game, the controller falling from his hands as he sat up straight, his eyes darting around the room. He listened intently, trying to discern the source of the noise, but there was only silence. Eoin shook his head. "Fuckin' paranoid eejit."

He settled back into the game, but a few minutes later, another noise startled him. This time, it sounded like something had fallen over in the hallway outside. Eoin paused the game again, his hands shaking slightly as he strained to hear anything else. But once again, there was nothing.

This pattern repeated itself a few more times, with each interruption making Eoin increasingly agitated. Finally, after a loud thump against the apartment door, Eoin threw his hands up in frustration.

"I'm too fuckin' stoned for this shit," he grumbled, tossing the controller onto the couch.

He stood up, swaying slightly as the effects of the joint hit him full force. Eoin stumbled toward the bedroom, his eyes heavy with exhaustion and the desire to escape the unsettling noises. He collapsed onto the bed without bothering to remove his clothes or turn off the light. Within moments, he was asleep, the sounds of the apartment fading away as he drifted off into a dreamless slumber.

———

Brendan shifted in the passenger seat of Tracy's car as they drove along a country road, heading to the party she had been cryptic about all week. Brendan inferred from her hints that it was a type of sex party, although the specifics remained mysterious.

"Here we are!" Tracy exclaimed as they pulled into a wide opening. A large wrought iron gate opened automatically, granting them access to a short driveway leading up to a luxurious two-story house. The sight of the other cars already parked there, many of them luxury vehicles with drivers, impressed Brendan.

He glanced down at his own clothing, feeling slightly out

of place. "I might be a tad underdressed," he said, a hint of uncertainty in his voice.

Tracy smirked, her eyes glinting with mischief. "Don't worry, you won't be wearing them for long."

Brendan smiled in response, his mind immediately drifting to the concealed knife he had brought along for his plans with Tracy later that night.

They exited the car and walked toward the door, the anticipation building with each step. At the imposing double doors, Tracy turned to him and whispered, "I hope you like the taste of piss, Big Boy."

Brendan smiled back at her, not sure he'd heard her right, but before he could ask, someone opened the doors inward and beckoned them through. *What the fuck have I gotten myself into?*

CHAPTER 39
LILLIAN

Lillian slammed the front door behind her, the sound echoing through the empty house. She leaned against the wood, her chest heaving with the force of her breathing. The image of Gabriel with that other woman burned in her mind, searing her heart with its cruel betrayal.

A scream tore from Lillian's throat, raw and primal. It shattered the silence, the anguish in her voice reverberating off the walls. She screamed again, pouring all her pain and rage into the sound until her throat was hoarse and her lungs burned.

Lillian's legs gave out, and she slid to the floor, her back pressed against the door. Sobs wracked her body, tears streaming down her face as she wrapped her arms around herself. The perfect future she had envisioned with Gabriel crumbled before her eyes, the shards of their shattered relationship cutting deep into her soul.

She curled in on herself, her forehead pressed to her knees as she wept. The tears soaked through her jeans, but Lillian barely noticed. The pain in her heart consumed her, drowning out everything else. She had given Gabriel everything, trusted him completely, and he had thrown it all away for a moment of fleeting pleasure.

Lillian's sobs echoed through the empty house, the mournful sound of heartbreak and despair. She rocked back and forth, her fingers digging into her arms as she tried to hold herself together. But the pain was too much, the betrayal too deep. She felt like she was coming apart at the seams, her world unravelling with each gasping breath.

Time lost all meaning for Lillian, lost in her grief. The screwdriver she had used to kill the woman lay forgotten on the floor beside her. Her mind reeled, replaying every moment of her relationship with Gabriel, searching for signs she had missed, clues that could have warned her of his infidelity.

But there was nothing. Just the cold, hard truth of his betrayal, shattering the illusion of their perfect love.

Lillian's sobs subsided, leaving her hollow and numb. She stared blankly at the wall, her eyes red and swollen. The house felt too big, too empty without Gabriel's presence. But now, even the thought of him made her stomach churn with revulsion.

She allowed herself to wallow in her misery, to feel the full weight of Gabriel's betrayal. She had loved him with every fibre of her being, and now that love lay in ruins at her feet.

———

Time passed. Lillian knew she would have to face the world eventually, to pick up the pieces of her shattered life and move on. Then another voice surfaced from her subconscious. *Do I?* The thought took her by surprise, but to her grieving, broken state of mind, it offered her a solution.

Lillian rose slowly from her place on the floor, a sense of renewed purpose filling her, albeit a fatalistic one. She made her way to the bathroom, each step deliberate and heavy with the weight of her decision. Turning on the faucet, she watched as the steaming water filled the bathtub, the rising steam obscuring her reflection in the mirror.

As the tub filled, Lillian retrieved the antique straight razor she had bought from a thrift store for just this sort of occasion. It felt cold and heavy in her hand, contrasting with the heat of the bathwater. She placed it on a small side table within arm's reach of the tub, her fingers lingering on the smooth handle for a moment before pulling away.

Lillian walked into the living room, her bare feet padding softly against the hardwood floor. She turned on the stereo, and the dulcet tones of the song 'Gabriel' by Lamb floated through the house, the haunting melody a fitting soundtrack to her despair. As the music filled the air, Lillian returned to the bathroom, each note a painful reminder of the love she had lost.

Standing before the bathtub, Lillian stripped off her clothing, letting each garment fall to the floor in a crumpled heap. She stepped into the hot water, the heat enveloping her body like a comforting embrace. She sank down into the tub, the water rising to her chest as she leaned back against the porcelain, her eyes closing as the music washed over her.

CHAPTER 40
EPILOGUE: THE END OF DAYS

illian held her breath, her body completely still, and focused the binoculars on the approaching car. It was too distant to discern any features, but she could tell it was a black car, possibly old-fashioned. Isn't everything old-fashioned now? What interested her was the enormous dark cloud of swirling nightmare that pursued the vehicle. *Maybe it only seems like it's chasing it*, she thought. Even though she couldn't hear the hunting horn or the screams of the damned, their echoes lingered in her mind. She shivered.

She heard Brendan approach but didn't take her eyes from the distant scene.

"We have trouble to the east," he said.

"Johners?"

"No. That fucking shadow that's herding your collection." Brendan's voice gave no hint that he had once come close to joining said collection. It didn't surprise her. He was a man of few words, preferring to let his actions do the talking.

"That can wait," she said, handing him the binoculars and pointing in the direction of the approaching vehicle. "We have a bigger problem."

Brendan focused in and swore. "For fuck's sake! Coming right for us."

"Looks like it."

"Huh," said Brendan, frowning slightly. He handed Lillian the binoculars. "They've stopped."

Lillian accepted them and watched as two figures exited the vehicle - one tall, one shorter. The tall one opened the passenger door and retrieved something. A child! The couple and child started out on foot directly toward them. "We have to pick them up." She lowered the binoculars and noticed Brendan's questioning look. "If that thing is pursuing them, maybe we can redirect it."

Brendan was already nodding, a broad grin plastered across his face. "I know just the place to send it."

———

Within the swirling cloud of nightmare, the Left Hand of Balor watched the family exit the horseless carriage and proceed on foot. He stood atop a writhing mass of Balor's minions, maintaining balance only through the staff's power. The same power kept the wailing shadows that swirled around him at bay. His long grey hair and beard moved as though in a slight breeze, as did his dark coat. His hand tightly grasped the twisted shaft of the staff, the sensation of its rough surface providing a sense of stability as the dark stone at its top throbbed in harmony with his own pulse.

Soon!

Yes, soon. Was that him or the other? He could no longer tell where his own thoughts ended and the other's began. It felt like an eternity had passed since they first met. No, not an eternity, but longer than the span of a single man's existence.

Ahead, his quarry stopped. Another carriage pulled up in a cloud of dust and ushered them in. Then the second carriage sped away to the east.

The Left Hand of Balor pulled power from the staff and willed the immense cloud to turn in the new direction. He couldn't, wouldn't, let them escape. Between them, they held the key to his redemption.

————

Brendan steered the car toward the town's eastern suburbs as the man in the back cast worried looks behind them. The woman fussed over the child, a girl of two or three as far as he could guess. The girl looked sick, feverish.

"It's turning," said the man.

"Fuck," said the woman.

Brendan gave the car more gas. That was about the closest he'd ever got to one of those damned clouds, and he was pushing the car hard to make distance on the thing.

"Is she okay?" he asked.

The woman didn't reply, but the man chimed in. "She will be."

"Fair enough." Brendan was doubtful, but he kept his opinion to himself. Folks died from all sorts of mundane things these days.

"Does this thing move any faster, friend?" The man smiled to take the edge off his words, but Brendan noted the strain in the man's eyes.

"This is as fast as she goes, I'm afraid," Brendan shrugged apologetically.

"It's gaining on us," said the woman.

"Fuck!" Brendan exclaimed. He wasn't cursing at the cloud. Ahead of them, the road ended in a barricade of recently erected burnt-out vehicles and debris. "Those fucking cunts!"

Brendan slammed on the brakes, the car skidding to a halt in a cloud of dust. He wrenched the steering wheel, spinning the vehicle around to face the oncoming threat. The dark mass filled the road, spilling into the fields on either side, an unstoppable force bearing down upon them.

"Fuck," Brendan muttered, his knuckles white as he gripped the wheel. There was nowhere to go, no escape from the impending doom.

From the backseat, the man spoke, his voice tight with fear, "Niamh..."

The woman, Niamh, replied with a determined edge, "Hold on, Jack." She reached into her bag and pulled out a large, leatherbound tome. The book looked ancient, its cover worn and cracked with age.

Brendan glanced in the rearview mirror, incredulous. *Who the hell reads at a time like this?* But his thoughts were cut short as Niamh chanted in a language he had never heard before, guttural and primal. The words warped the surrounding air.

Brendan's eyes widened as he caught sight of Niamh's reflection. Her eyes had turned a deep, unsettling onyx, devoid of any humanity. She met his gaze in the mirror, her voice rising to a commanding shout, "DRIVE!"

The demonic command jolted through Brendan like an electric shock. His foot slammed down on the accelerator, the tires screeching as the car lurched forward. The engine roared, propelling them straight toward the heart of the swirling cloud.

Brendan's heart pounded in his chest, adrenaline surging through his veins. He had no idea what Niamh's chanting would do, but he had no choice except to trust in her power. As they hurtled toward the darkness, Brendan gritted his teeth, bracing himself for the impact.

He held his breath as the car plunged into the heart of the unnatural cloud, the swirling darkness engulfing them. The vehicle shuddered and shook as if caught in the grip of an otherworldly force. Through the chaos, he could hear Niamh's chanting, her words a flimsy barricade against the darkness.

Black shapes abruptly emerged from the bleak greyness, their forms twisting and writhing as they surrounded the car. They pressed against the windows and doors, their fingers clawing at the glass and metal, seeking entrance. Brendan's breath caught in his throat as he watched the creatures' relentless assault, their hunger palpable.

But Niamh's power pushed back, a shimmering barrier forming around the car, repelling the creatures' advances. The shapes recoiled, their shrieks of frustration piercing the air.

Then, a figure emerged from the darkness, standing before them. It was a man with long grey hair and a full beard, his eyes glinting with cruel intelligence. In his hands, he held a twisted staff, the black stone at its top pulsing with an eerie power.

In the darkness, the car felt suspended and frozen in space. The man raised his staff, and a wave of energy surged forth, colliding with Niamh's barrier. The two forces battled for dominance, the air crackling with their power.

Brendan watched in horror as Niamh's strength waned, her chanting faltering. With a final, devastating blow, the man's power shattered Niamh's defences and she slumped forward, unconscious.

The creatures surged ahead, their hunger renewed. They tore at the car, their claws rending metal and glass. The doors twisted outward, the windows shattering, leaving Brendan and the others exposed to the horrors that awaited them.

But then, an otherworldly scream rang out, piercing the darkness. It came from the girl, no longer feverish, her eyes glowing with a golden light. She held out her hand before her, the gesture unnervingly unchildlike.

A woman's voice, ancient and powerful, spoke through her, "Begone."

In an instant, the creatures vanished, their forms dissipating. The car lurched forward, the engine roaring to life, and slammed into the grey-haired man sending him tumbling to the ground, his staff clattering beside him.

And then, just as suddenly as it had begun, it was over. The car burst through the other side of the cloud, emerging into the clear air. Brendan exhaled sharply, his hands trembling on the wheel. He glanced in the rearview mirror, half-expecting to see the dark mass still pursuing them, but there was nothing but road and the crumpled form of the grey-haired man behind them.

Brendan climbed out of the battered car and stepped back from it. He looked from the damaged car to the man on the road and back again.

"Well, fuck me."

THANKS FOR READING

Thanks for reading The House of Marionettes. I hope you enjoyed it and will consider leaving an honest review on Amazon, Goodreads, or wherever else you feel comfortable with.

As an indie author, reviews are one of the best ways to raise visibility and slay those algorithmic monsters.

Best,

B.C.

ACKNOWLEDGMENTS

I would like to thank the following individuals for their support and contributions to this project:

My family, once again for their patience and understanding of this obsession of mine.

My editor, Dani, who did an amazing job, making what you hold in your hands so much better.

My beta readers, Kate and Andy, who provided excellent feedback on an early draft and made the story make sense where sense was lacking.

Last but not least, the reader, for taking the time to read another one of my stories. Without you, I'd just be having conversations with myself.

Thanks to all of you!

B.C. Hollywood

August, 2024

RED JACKET: A PREQUEL TO SHADOW APOCALYPSE

Available to newsletter subscribers soon at www. bchollywood.com/newsletter .

HELLFIRE

Available October 2024

ABOUT THE AUTHOR

B.C. Hollywood is an Irish author of dark fiction, fantasy, and horror. He spends much of his spare time battering raw story ideas into shapelier form.

He writes novels, short stories, flash fiction, screenplays, poetry, and tabletop games. He is the author of *The Darkle Chronicles* series of apocalyptic stories of which *The House of Marionettes* is book three.

To connect with B.C. and for news of his upcoming titles, you can check out his website at www.bchollywood.com, join his newsletter, and follow his Facebook author page.

The release of the fourth book in *The Darkle Chronicles* series, *Shadows Rising,* is scheduled for early 2025.